The Fis

THE FISH TANK:
AND OTHER SHORT STORIES

Maria Elena Alonso-Sierra

Cover design by Scott Carpenter
Print Edition:
ISBN: 10: 09982574-0-0
ISBN-13: 978-0-9982574-0-2

OTHER WORKS BY
MARIA ELENA ALONSO-SIERRA

Hanging Softly in the Night: A Detective Nick Larson Novel
Mirror, Mirror: A Prequel Detective Nick Larson Short Story
Retribution Served
The Book of Hours
The Coin

Soul Songs is dedicated to all my fellow Cubans, here and abroad.

We have survived and triumphed—despite suffering atrocities at the hands of the brutal Castroist regime.

TABLE OF CONTENTS

Section 1: Note from the Author   9

Section 2: For the Fun of Writing (Just Because)   11
Jerry's Gift   13
Rites of Passage   17

Section 3: Soul Songs (Stories from the Cuban Diaspora)   23
The Fish Tank—Finalist Win at Carried in Waves Contest   25
Bubbles Don't Bring Smiles   33
Lullaby   51
Another Day in the Life of Benito José Fuentes   57

Section 4: Prologues   67
Into the Light   69
Mirror, Mirror—A Detective Nick Larson Story   85

Section 5: The End   107
Everyone's a Critic   109

A NOTE FROM THE AUTHOR...

I never considered myself to be a short story writer. As a matter of fact, I steered away from this type of narrative simply because I believed it was a very difficult medium to write in.

And I was correct.

Novels give you leeway to explore, to expand, to take liberties. You don't have to worry about length. Characters, conflict, plot can be developed slowly, differently.

With short stories, a writer has to gut punch the reader immediately. The story must be told within certain parameters. Characters must be real from the first words spoken. Conflict must be intense, almost at the climax point, and the resolution finished sometimes subtly, sometimes shockingly, and sometimes not necessarily as a happily ever after.

I wrote my first short story while getting my Master's degree, but I stopped because life got in the way. Years later, I decided to publish my novel, *The Coin*, and to write its sequel, *The Book of Hours*. But always, in the back of my mind, I wanted to do something about the short stories I'd written and, maybe, expand the repertoire, especially the stories from my childhood, my experiences as a Cuban exile.

This collection came to fruition after one of my short stories, "The Fish Tank", won a finalist spot in the Carried in Waves contest at the University of Cork, Ireland. That pushed me to finally compile what I'd written and to write the rest of the stories roiling in my mind (I still have a few more to tell, but that is for a future collection).

I divided the collection into four sections, which I believe are self-explanatory: For the Fun of Writing (Just Because), Soul Songs (Stories from the Cuban Diaspora), Prologues (prequel stories from upcoming novels), and The End, a short, short-short piece of author whimsy.

On the second section, Soul Songs...

Those stories were difficult to write. Soul-tearing. Each one contains one, or several events I personally experienced. And trust me, even when those incidents happened close to what feels (and is) a lifetime ago, the fear, the pain, the longing, the melancholy of turmoil experienced, things lost, and inevitable change remains. I never suspected creating the short stories would tear at the scab protecting a deep wound I still harbor in my heart, one that will not quite properly heal.

As always, I want to thank Scott Carpenter for his wonderful work on the book cover and Anita Mumm for sharing her wonderful editorial expertise.

Another thing...

This collection was a labor of love.

I hope you love it as much as I loved writing it.

Maria Elena Alonso-Sierra

FOR THE FUN OF WRITING
(Just Because)

JERRY'S GIFT

PEELING paint, outside and in, no wall and no ceiling immune to the wrinkling effect of age, no surface worse off than another.

Maureen took the exfoliated, ivory-colored flakes in stride, dismissing the dusting in her hair, her clothes, and her life as a bad case of temporary dandruff. But the flaking walls of her great-grandfather's house, like her life, would shortly be renovated as soon as she negotiated an equitable price for Jerry's gift.

Damn satisfying.

The slanting sun warmed her skin to a faint blush as she sat on the veranda, the breeze pregnant with the scents of pine and rose. Maureen loved this southwest corner of the porch. The air served as walls and nature replaced the lack of decor. Every afternoon, after she stopped the refurbishing, she made a pitcher of lemonade and sat facing the eighty-year-old maple trees at the edge of the property.

Her ritual.

Her space.

Her world.

She laughed, and the soft sound mingled with the strident chirp of the cicada. She flexed her toes against the bare boards, set her rocking chair in lazy arcs and, without haste, scooped shipwrecked paint chips from her lemonade. She filled her mouth with citrus coolness and reveled as the liquid trickled slowly, very slowly down her throat.

Jerry thought he'd won. He believed that because he'd manipulated things so Maureen would be left with a miserable lump sum of cumulative income from the divorce settlement. The X-factor, she had called it—X as a percentage of their years of marriage subtracted from Jerry's X productive years as a lawyer.

A pittance.

But Maureen hadn't complained. Didn't complain. She was content.

She smiled. An image of her ex-husband, smirking as he roamed the thin streets of Europe with his newest bimbo, Grace, flashed through her mind. Maureen could easily imagine him gloating, believing he'd put her in her place—after all, she was a nobody, from a nobody family, back to a nobody ex-wife. Never mind if she had spent the greater part of her youth supporting him while he studied corporate law. Never mind if his pedigreed family had disowned him for the duration of their marriage. Never mind, either, if she had spent the last three years molding herself physically and socially to mirror Jerry's definition of a wife, before getting fed up and filing for a divorce. In the end, none of her efforts had mattered. Maureen hadn't been flashy enough for his career, or enough of an ego boost for a superstar attorney. When she had finally served him papers, Jerry's relief had been palpable, the document some sort of divine sign validating his voyage of self-discovery, giving him carte blanche to hoard more mistresses than previously.

Maureen set her rocker in motion once more, enjoying how the movement displaced the air and cooled the skin around her neck. Who would have thought, after the nasty divorce proceedings, that Jerry's last act would be one of generosity? A satisfied chuckle vibrated within her chest and the air stirred, mixing the scents of pine and mossy earth around the veranda. The shifting maple leaves captured the light and winked like jewels against the magenta sky.

Jewels. Such an appropriate symbol, Maureen thought, one worthy of a liquor-free toast.

"Here's to ex-husbands." She raised her glass in tribute. "And their need to find themselves."

Several paint chips spiraled their way to the ground. She drank more deeply and patted the square, black velvet pouch riding her lap. She should thank Jerry for his impatience and for his compulsion to prove his male prowess. His behavior had been her saving grace. By this time tomorrow, the two-carat diamond cufflinks, the ruby and diamond earrings and matching pendant, the 18K gold and sapphire bracelet and ring, and the brooch with an emerald as wide as her thumbnail's matrix, Jerry's pride, his family heirlooms, would be dismantled, cut, redesigned, and sold. Because he had been in such a hurry to discover Europe and plunder the depths of his latest sex toy, he had rushed to retrieve the jewelry pouch from the safe deposit box a couple of hours before his flight, without inspecting its contents. He'd forgotten he'd stashed her jewelry together with his late grandmother's the year before. And because Jerry had been drooling over the finality of their divorce, once he'd delivered Maureen's pitiful cachet of pearl necklaces, bracelets, and emerald teardrop earrings to her lawyer, Maureen had been handed an unexpected bonus, *gratis*, free of liability and reprisal.

Maureen lifted the velvet pouch and cradled it in her palm. Its weight satisfied her sense of contentment and justice served. And if the mistake were ever discovered, all roads would lead to her ex-husband. Maureen had not been near the bank, nor was her signature anywhere in any document linking her to that safe deposit box. Never had been. Jerry's trust had never extended to include Maureen as co-signer in the safe deposit bank account.

His loss. Her gain.

Gravel crunched. Maureen's visitor parked next to her RV. With lemonade glass in one hand and the jewelry pouch tucked in the other, Maureen stood. She dusted her hair, smiled, and waited for the jeweler to reach her.

RITES OF PASSAGE

"MOM. Mo-om! Let me go on that one. Please?"

My son's excited voice warns me. My eyes confirm the challenge is even worse. The massive roller coaster he's pointing at is huge; the screams from its riders are sharp, even in the surrounding racket.

"Are you sure you want to get on that thing?" I ask, my apprehension rising.

"Oh, yeah." He scoots over to a notice posted at the entrance of the ride and practically merges into it. His hand draws an imaginary line from his head to the wide line painted at the top. It lands about two inches higher. "This year I'm tall enough. I can really go on this thing." He rushes back, grabs my waist, and gives it a quick squeeze. "Please, please, please, pretty please?"

I know I'm the intrepid kind, but I don't like modern roller coasters—well, not all of them. The huge plunges and the resulting free-falls from these new, state-of-the-art thrill rides do not correlate with my definition of excitement. They remind me of another ride, more traumatic, more devastating. I stare at the coiling metal structure, appropriately baptized *Viper*. From my angle, it looks bigger than Mount Everest and as nasty as the snake it's named after.

I gulp and turn to my husband for help, but his expression signals he's not going to be very cooperative. He thinks my phobia is exaggerated, female histrionics, controllable if I put my mind to it. Not like his—physical, debilitating, masculinity subtracted. Only, I know better. In emphasis, my husband shakes his head once more and mimics gagging expressions. My oldest son, who suffers from a middle ear malady, hangs on to his father's side like a leech, his mutinous expression one of, *You'll never get me riding on that thing.*

"Well, I guess you're tall enough to ride—"

"He's not going in any ride alone."

My husband's tone is emphatic, his eyes disappointed at my easy capitulation, in me.

"I can't believe you're even considering it, Kate. Bryan's too young to ride without adult supervision. You know that."

"Jack, you promised he could ride the roller coasters. Alone. He's tall enough now. These people are more safety conscious than I am."

"I never said he could ride alone. He's too young to be responsible." His eyes lift, as if asking the sky for patience. "I can't believe I'm having this discussion with you. You're the adult here."

I want to slap my husband. He's always using his escape clauses, caging me into a corner, forcing me to decide, to capitulate to his logic. And the frustrating part in all this is that, if I agree or disagree, it ends up always being my fault, or my lack of sense, or my smothering sensibility.

"Besides, nothing's going to happen to Bryan if he doesn't ride this thing. It won't be the end of the world." My husband's eyes soften. I recognize paternal condescension in them. "Why don't we go catch the animal show?"

I stare at my husband. "The park closes after the animal show."

"So?"

I look at my youngest. His almond eyes are locked on my face. He looks like a puppy dog begging for a treat, suspecting he won't get one, and trying not to be too disappointed. It wouldn't be the first time.

"I'll ride with you," I tell him, knowing I'm going to regret it. Yet, I can't trample my youngest son's yen for adventure. Not because of my fears, or my husband's cowardice.

"You're going to regret this, Kate."

"Let's go, Bryan."

"All right!"

Taking no chances, my son grabs my hand and drags me through the entrance.

We rush inside, the path leading to the ride winding and winding around the foot of the metallic monster. The pace my son sets leaves me breathless. Finally, we catch up with the shortest line in roller coaster history. My hands begin to sweat. I know I'm hyperventilating. I silently scold myself. I've been on other roller coasters with my son. How bad could this one be? This isn't an elevator, falling and jerking to a stop every couple of inches. It isn't a metal cave trapping me for hours on end.

The roller coaster roars past our left at a dizzying speed.

My mental reply is, *Oh, shit.*

My son stands awestruck, nervous, excited.

"Da bomb," he says. "Way cool."

My legs start faltering as we approach the point of no return. I lock my knees and manage a couple of steps.

"Are you sure you want to get on?" I ask again. The first plunge looks gigantic. I try to forget the claustrophobia, the jolts, the elevator doors stuck open, a faded number 6 dancing in match light, framed by gaping steel jaws.

My son suddenly stops his excited bouncing and turns to face me.

"Are you scared, Mom?"

My first instinct is to blurt out the truth: *Yes, son. I'm scared spitless.* My second thought is that I'd never impart my fear on my sons. It's my problem, not theirs, and I'm not about to break that habit by telling them about the New York blackout, about getting stuck on my apartment building's elevator, alone, a matchbook my only comfort. Four hours in a vertically sliding coffin. My husband dismisses my fear—it happened long ago. I should have gotten over it by now. I look at my son again. How can I spoil his first experience in a grown-up roller coaster ride? After all, this is his rite of passage.

"Nah," I answer instead, and take another deep breath.

"Are you sure, Mom? If you really don't want to go, I understand."

I pat his nose with my finger and smile. "I'm game, if you are."

He hugs me tightly. "Thanks, Mom."

Pausing at the turnstile while my son rushes through, I glance at the rotating metal fingers and then up at what can be seen of the ride. I hesitate, my gut wrenching in a nervous spasm. *I can do this. I can.* I slide reluctantly through, my stomach muscles clenched, fear riding my throat. Up ahead, my son heads for the waiting area marked "first car riders only." I rush after him, grab him by the T-shirt, and pull him back.

"Oh, no. Not on the first seats."

"Aw, Mom."

"No. Way."

I steer him to another waiting area. He looks disappointed but doesn't complain. For now, it's the best he'll get.

Our turn arrives too quickly. A silent, apathetic teenager opens the gate and points to our seats. With a similar air of bored monotony, another teenager imprisons us under foam-padded steel hooks. My son strangles the padded metal handlebars in his euphoria and bounces like a springboard on his seat. I check the bars securing me in place for the tenth time and grab on for dear life.

The roller coaster jerks to a start. We roll up. I look around and then decide against it. My stomach lurches. The climb doesn't seem to stop. As we clank higher, I wonder when the heck this is going to start. Another internal voice nastily reminds me that what we climb is what we plunge.

My saliva dries in my mouth.

By now, halfway up, the twilight breeze feels cool. I whisk off my baseball cap as well as my son's, secure both under my behind, and try not to dwell on the drop ahead.

"Look, look, Mom," he shouts, even though I can hear him perfectly. "We're flying."

He stretches both arms out and flaps them like a bird. I grab on to both and slam them back on the rods.

"Stop that," I order, trying to ignore the shrinking view below me. "Just hold on." I turn to face the looming sky and follow my own advice. But my stomach is knotted like a brick, and my entire body is rippling with tremors. I pluck at my temporary, steel-fork prison bars wanting to merge into them, to become as rigid as them. I want out and can't.

Finally, the roller coaster reaches the summit. The sky welcomes us. We hover for a second, for an instant. I look down.

Oh. My. God.

Gravity shoves us. The roller coaster plunges. Free fall grabs hold of my body. My stomach compresses, heaves. We plunge. The wind slaps my exposed skin. My facial muscles ripple in tiny waves. My stomach feels glued to my mouth. I huddle to see if the nauseous effect gets better. No go.

We take a curve. My son's legs slam into my body. I strangle the foam-padded rods. He's laughing. I'm screaming. We turn the other way. I'm compressed against my prison bars. By now my skin is vibrating. My hair lashes my eyes, ears, and mouth like a thousand tiny whips. My mind screams frantically, *I want to get off! I want to get off!*

My screams get louder.

We lurch. The roller coaster roars up another huge hill. It dives. The wheels underneath thunder, the wind above carries my screams. We whiz into a tighter curve. Faster. Faster. We zoom upside down. My behind gets plastered against the seat. We twirl at impossible angles like training astronauts. My son leans forward into the G-force. I huddle even closer into my seat, my arms numb from grabbing on. We zip up another little mountain. We roar back down. We jerk. We finally slow down. The roller coaster glides home.

The Beast rests.

"Awesome," my son whoops. He shoves the steel hooks from his body and jumps out onto the platform. I want to bend and kiss the ground.

"Mom, wasn't that the most awesomest thing? Wasn't it, huh?"

I drop the baseball cap onto his head and take a huge breath to steady my stomach. My hands are trembling and my body wants to go into convulsive tremors.

"Yeah," I croak.

"Can we do it again? Please, please?"

"Sweetie, I—"

"Mom, please. This is our last day here. It's almost closing time. And Daddy won't come with me. He never does. Says it's stupid to do these things, but that's because he pukes all the time. I think he's afraid."

I look at my son in wonder. Out of the mouths of babes...

"Please, Mom. You're the only one that shares these things with me. Please, Mom, please?"

Near us, toward the exit, I see my husband waving impatiently at us.

"Come on," he yells. "I want to see the tech exhibit before the park closes."

I look into my son's pleading eyes and weigh two minutes of fear against his disillusionment. I mentally brace myself and say, "Okay."

He hugs me tightly and gives me a whopping kiss.

"You're the bestest Mom that ever lived on the planet. I love you."

I lift his cap, rumple his hair, and drop a kiss on his forehead.

"Yeah. I love you, too."

Riding high on a wave of euphoria, he waves at his father and zips back through the entrance.

"Guys, get over here," my husband yells. "Guys. What are you doing?"

I wave. "We're going to ride this again."

My husband's jaw drops. I smile.

I follow my son at a slower pace, nursing my shaken courage, persuading myself the second time around won't be so bad.

Yeah, right.

With eyes brimming with happiness and face flushed with excitement, my son rushes back to me. He hugs me fiercely once again and takes my hand. I squeeze his and follow him along the endless loops and through the turnstile.

With a heartfelt sigh, I stand in line again.

SOUL SONGS

(Stories from the Cuban Diaspora)

THE FISH TANK*

(*2015 Finalist at Carried in Waves Contest from
the University of Cork, Ireland)

MATILDE sat beside her mother in the same manner, the same chair, and in the same corner as an hour ago, the corrugated vinyl of the seat cushion hot against her small thighs. Her back created a perfect parallel to the chair's backrest barely two inches behind her, and the organza skirt she wore, a faded green, frothed around her legs, its color a pitiful contrast against the vivid white petticoat underneath. She tried not to move, unlike the other adults inside the room who shifted nervously in kaleidoscope patterns. Her doll also mimicked her posture, its weight barely denting the rigidity of her own starched green dress.

Matilde raised her legs without jostling the doll on her lap and studied the top of her black vinyl, ballerina pumps. If she stared hard enough into the tiny dark mirrors, she'd see a distorted, shadowy image of her lace-fringed bobby socks reflecting off the shine. She lowered her legs and pointed her feet, testing the length of the void beneath them until the very tip of her shoes patted the mottled terrazzo floor. This action distracted her from the queasiness in her stomach. She felt boxed in by the three walls of military green and the one of bulletproof glass, but she didn't complain. Her mother had warned against the dangers of fidgeting, of playing. Attention must not be drawn.

Period.

Her stomach disagreed.

Matilde sensed her mother's glance and watched as she opened her vinyl pillbox purse. Was her mother scavenging for her favorite violet-flavored candy? She hoped so. The imported pastilles, little lilac-colored squares filled with French fragrance, had been rationed like stolen treasure for the past year, and each had been carefully quartered to extend the pleasure. Only three remained. Now, careful so the wrapper wouldn't disintegrate in her fingers, Matilde saw her mother separate one purple pill within the protective shadows of the purse.

"Suck on this, *mi amor*." Her mother pressed the square candy, intact, against Matilde's sweaty palm. "I'll see about lunch."

Her mother's hushed voice barely filtered down to Matilde's level. For the past year, conversations, transformed into nervous whispers, were infused by an undertow of fear and despair. The whispers had gotten even softer since arriving here at *la pecera*, the airport's holding pen. A fish tank, her mother had said—a temporary prison quarantining them like diseased animals. Her mother didn't like the room. Matilde didn't either.

Her mother's soft touch lingered on her cheek, and Matilde leaned into the caress with a slight tilt to her head. Warmth dissipated as her mother stood and retreated, the muted sound of her high heels picking at the dirty terrazzo floor.

More whispers.

Trying not to attract notice, Matilde deposited the square candy on her tongue, caressed and spread the flavor ever so softly around her mouth. Her eyelids drooped, hiding her gaze as it darted from object to object in this stuffy room, warm despite the cranky air conditioning. The mold stain, at the bottom corner of the wall facing her, had mottled the paint like chicken pox and played peek-a-boo with the ugly, brown orthopedic shoes of the old lady sitting on the couch. A thin fault line marred the dirty pumpkin-colored cushions of the misused couch, the gray clumps of wadding underneath trying to break free. The important lady, an actress Matilde had been told, so pretty in her black chemise, matching nylons, and high heels, circled and circled in the middle of their enclosed space, a human merry-go-round going nowhere.

Her saliva, now full of a violet richness, calmed her stomach and her nervousness. She heard her mother speak in agitated whispers as more adults gravitated toward her. The important lady joined the group, her fresh dress a stark contrast to her mother's tired one. Matilde wanted to sigh but only exhaled quietly. The simple, strapless, blue cotton sundress her mother wore looked like a washed sky, but it was starched crisp, and it was clean. Her mother fiercely insisted that dignity and cleanliness must prevail, especially during these terrible times. Besides, wearing their good clothes would only focus unwelcome attention on them. That mustn't happen.

The adult's whispers solidified in the stale air, crashing and receding against Matilde's ears.

". . . can't hand out food."

"Nothing. Left her with nothing."

"Young man, conscripted. Only fourteen."

"His father . . . Oh, God!"

"Betrayed. Her own daughter."

". . .wounded, trying to stow aboard the plane."

"Twenty years. For what?"

"—cursing the official."

". . . found string of pearls . . . in lining of suitcase."

"Strip-searched. In front of husband."

"Bastards."

"Bastards."

Matilde smoothed the cool velvet of her doll's dress with the fastidious precision of an adult, careful not to crease the blue fabric, adjusting the skirt just so. It was a beautiful Snow White doll, crafted in Switzerland, with a smooth porcelain face, round innocent eyes, rosy cheeks, and a pout for a smile. A family heirloom, handed down from mother to daughter for four generations.

Matilde cradled her doll, softly pressing her against her bosom, and sang to it, her words barely a breeze in the recycled air. She missed her toys, her dresses, and her beautiful illustrated books. She missed her pink ballerina wallpaper, her bicycle, and her creaky rocking chair. But these were sad times, her mother kept saying. That was why everything that was portable had been smuggled out of their home, distributed to the few relatives who insisted on staying in Cuba. Matilde, even yesterday, had sat on top of her mother's silver flatware set in the back seat of their black Fiat. The box, cradling the silverware, had dug into the back of her exposed thighs, while the guard, posted at the periphery of their neighborhood a year ago, had meticulously searched the car's trunk. The man had never suspected that Matilde's petticoat concealed a silver hoard underneath a layer of fluffy tulle and itchy fabric. And with a final *buchito de café*, one her mother had thoughtfully brought for the guard in an aluminum thermos, they had outwitted the *miliciano*.

Matilde's curious eyes swept around the room once more but stopped short of the daunting glass barrier on her left. If she focused on the transparent wall sealing them in, she would see her ghostly image mirrored back, fragmented by the human traffic on the other side. She concentrated on a single drop of condensation weeping down the slick surface, and realized the shoes were not there. She wanted to smile, but didn't, just in case. It was so horrible when he was there, the man who observed them intermittently, his gaze calculating, radiating a palpable, hypnotic malice. When he stood on the other side of the cold glass, his shadow crept across the pane as if searching for a victim. Once found, it would absorb and digest their ghostly reflections like Jonah's whale. Nobody from the group ever noticed—nobody but her.

And each time he stood there, someone was taken out, never to return.

A shudder rippled over Matilde, but she immediately stilled. The man with the empty stare might be out there, waiting beyond the glass, undetected, targeting their scraggly group once more, his face devoid of humanity, his glance hungry for them.

She must not fidget. She must stay still.

Matilde's mother returned and sat noiselessly beside her.

"No lunch now," her mother whispered close to her ear. "Can you wait, *mi amor*?"

Matilde nodded. Her mother gathered her in, squeezing Matilde's shoulders until they folded inward like an accordion.

"We'll eat on the airplane," she continued, her voice low, crooning almost. "The stewardess told me they have ham and eggs ready for us."

Matilde's mouth watered once more. They hadn't had the luxury of ham and eggs since the government had rationed food a year ago and restricted everything for everyone. Well, not everyone. Before he escaped after the *Playa Girón* invasion, Matilde remembered her father saying that the government bastards had plenty to eat. It was everyone else who didn't.

"Would you like that?" her mother asked.

Matilde nodded and barely smiled.

"I'd prefer a *tostada* and a Coke," she confessed. Freshly baked Cuban bread, cut thick and swimming with butter, was her favorite. So was the fizzy sweetness of the soft drink she loved. Her grandmother had always fed her that as an after-school snack. She hadn't had one for more than a year.

"We'll ask *Papi* to buy you some when we get to our new home."

Matilde snuggled closer to her mother. "Will we get there?"

Her mother squeezed Matilde's shoulder harder, but said nothing. She couldn't.

The brightness in the room dimmed. A shadow crept across Matilde's doll and she jerked, her heart thumping so hard, her dress front vibrated. She glanced through the glass barrier and saw the shoes, then the man. Matilde's small frame shuddered, rattling the doll on her lap. He was looking at her, his black eyes focused. From her angle, those black eyes seemed to devour instead of reflect images. Instinct tensed Matilde's small muscles for flight, but she didn't stir, nor did she move her doll. She only blinked. And the man, miraculously, didn't linger. He simply walked away, blending with the air and the outside world at the edge of the impenetrable glass.

Matilde stared until her eyes burned, but the man didn't return.

The only exit door in the room opened. A *miliciano* stepped in, his militia fatigues blending with the color on the walls. He jerked his head to the side, and his submachine gun twitched in the same direction.

"Out!" The *miliciano's* eyes razed the room. Head and gun jerked again. "Now."

Her mother helped Matilde straighten her skirt and petticoat, then weaved trembling fingers around Matilde's sweaty ones. Hand in hand they walked, their shoes placed softly on the hard floor. The important lady went across the threshold first, her head lifted, arrogant, defiant. The airline personnel went next, followed by the old people. No one was stopped. No one was detained. The group scurried along a windowless hallway to the only doors visible. Beyond the streaked door panes, Matilde could see a distorted image of the tarmac and the waiting airplane.

I'm going to see Papi.

She mustn't twitch, touch her skirt, or fidget now. She must be as quiet as a mouse.

The double doors opened. Sunlight overpowered the hallway. Matilde blinked and hugged her doll tighter.

The shadow surged, a dark force amid the scents of ripening guava, rich earth, airplane fumes, and humidity. The barrel of the *miliciano's* gun gated them back and Matilde whimpered. Her mother squeezed her hand. Her fingers paled as much as their faces.

He had come.

The man stood, feet braced, facing Matilde and her mother, studying them with analytical detachment. Matilde could hear her heart thumping inside her ears. Rivulets of sweat tickled her back. She wanted to step closer to her mother, but her small legs vibrated. If she moved, she would stumble and jostle her skirt.

"Pretty doll," the man said, his dark eyes huge, pupil and iris blending in an unforgiving black. His arm extended, a destructive tentacle toward Matilde. "Can I see it?"

Matilde's mother nudged her arm, her trembling smile a small reassurance. Instinctively, Matilde pressed her Snow White against her chest. It was her only toy, her most precious toy.

Matilde slowly extended her arm.

The man carefully dislodged the doll from her grasp and examined it as studiously as he had inspected them moments before. As Matilde watched, the man's lips curved in a brutal smile, a satisfied smile. He ripped the doll's clothing apart, tearing seams, ripping undergarments, sleeves, the pieces discarded like conquered confetti. He then quartered the doll, shaking the torso, digging inside for treasure as if the doll were a *piñata*.

Matilde watched in silence. Tears tripped and fell from her huge rounded eyes, her little hand strangling her mother's fingers. She didn't twitch, touch her skirt, or fidget. Matilde simply stood there in hopeless silence. No time for whispered prayers.

The man shook the doll one last time, inspected his handiwork, and extended the broken doll to Matilde, his face expressionless. What could have passed for regret flickered in the man's eyes before he turned, without rush, to disappear into the airport terminal.

The *miliciano* broke their inertia by pushing them forward and onto the plane. Inside, Matilde followed her mother to their seats and arranged her petticoat and skirt as fastidiously as before. The doors closed, sealing them inside. They waited. The propellers coughed, caught the wind, and roared.

The plane moved. It taxied forever, then gathered momentum, and lifted them to touch the sky. Matilde stared at her injured doll, touched her rent skirt with a finger. She then did the same to her own skirt and closed her eyes. Slowly at first, then more confidently, she caressed the green organza, trying to feel the treasure inside. Her finger glided over the cool material. No bumps, no change in smoothness, the double interfacing cradled inside the facing of her skirt providing the perfect camouflage for the booty inside—currency, hundreds of bills, washed to prevent crackling and discovery. Future hopes and dreams in soft, green dollar bills.

Matilde opened her eyes. She wiggled in her seat and tucked her legs under her. She leaned toward her mother and lifted her doll's broken body.

"*Mami*?" she asked, her voice loud, laced with hurt. "*Mami*, can we fix her?"

BUBBLES DON'T BRING SMILES

THE clack-clack of my father's Peugeot caught my attention, unlike the geometry lesson my tutor discussed in boring monotone.

"Now, Martica," my teacher said. "If a congruent angle—"

"*Coño!*"

My teacher stopped in mid-speech, startled. I chuckled at my father's heartfelt curse. A loud thud followed. A scrape. The car door slammed. More bangs followed, increased. My father's profanities got better and more colorful as he made his way across the garage.

"God damn it! She's going to get us killed," he shouted. A crash. "Silvia. *Mamá!*"

Listening to my father's chaotic approach as he navigated the obstacle course that was our garage, I empathized with his frustration. My grandmother, Abue Cachita, hoarded, the loot stockpiled in the most unexpected places inside our home. Before the revolution, my grandmother's compulsion to clip and accumulate buttons before discarding an old shirt, or her continuous demands that we wash and stack every empty glass jar of marmalade the family consumed, or her need to buy five packets of cooking lard instead of one, had not created any problems. Abue's eccentricity almost always elicited a pithy, *What do you expect? She's nearing sixty,* or brought on a fit of chuckles at family gatherings. But now, one-and-a-half years after the worst political debacle in Cuban history, her penchant to accumulate was downright dangerous.

The garage door slammed. My father appeared, suffocated. He focused on me and didn't acknowledge my tutor.

"Martica. Where's your mother?"

I gaped, shocked. My father never, ever had a hair out of place, or a wrinkled shirt, or stained shoes or pants. I stared from his dusty, perfed captoe Oxfords, to the sweat patches staining his underarms, to his hastily loosened tie, to his rumpled hair. The state of his hair truly captured my attention, cluing me to my father's emotional state.

"Martica!"

I pointed toward the kitchen doors through which my mother and grandmother had disappeared an hour ago, cooing over their most recent cachet of banned American products.

"In the laundry room," I answered.

"Silvia!" my father yelled and barged through the swinging doors into the kitchen.

"What do you think is going on?" I asked my tutor.

My teacher shook his head. Fascinated, I watched his upper lip distill sweat in drops that magnified his skin. His Adam's apple quivered and he couldn't decide whether to sit or stand, his body halfway out of his seat in a limbo of indecision.

I picked up my pencil and extended a bisecting angle on my notebook, drew additional tangents and shaded the spaces in between, careful not to utilize too much room on the notebook. Nineteen sixty-one was turning out to be a crappy year. My fifteenth birthday, precisely two months away in June, would be celebrated at home with a simple cake. And I didn't want a mere cake made from ground cassava flour that tasted flat. I didn't care if it was the only substitute available, or that we were lucky to get it twice a month from the son of a farmer who used to know a neighbor of my great-grandfather near Las Villas. I wanted my Cinderella ball. I wanted to emulate Audrey Hepburn as I had seen her in the movies, to walk through the receiving line, a princess in lace, with a tiara weaved into my hair, and a pink rose cradled in my gloved hands. I wanted what my mother and my grandmother had had. I wanted both the young men and the old to ogle, needed to feel my heart flutter as they watched my progress across the ballroom. I wanted to bask in the round-eyed astonishment of Jose Luis's sexy green eyes, to feel my stomach contract and my nerves tingle underneath my flesh as he witnessed my transformation from next-door caterpillar to desirable butterfly.

Unfortunately, unlike Cinderella, an evil troll had supplanted my fairy godmother. Jose Luis was gone, conscripted. Our gated beach community was under siege by human government drones planted with rifles at the entrance gate under orders to protect the recently acquired property of the state—namely everything we owned. Worse, my father's income from his tobacco plant, thanks to the government takeover, was now worth no more than a package of Chiclets.

"*Ay, Dios!*"

The force of my mother's wail made me jump. My tutor turned gray.

My father marched into the dining room, my mother close behind and as pale as my teacher. She looked like an opera singer in a mad scene, her hands clenched in her hair.

"Emilio, what are we going to do?"

"I don't know," my father said. "But you'd better come up with something. The random checks start in twenty minutes."

"If they find what we have, we'll be thrown in jail."

"Or killed by a firing squad," my grandmother added.

"*Mamá!*"

"Cachita!"

"Abue!"

"You're running like cockroaches sprayed with DDT," Abue Cachita said calmly. "Except Gustavo." She pointed to my teacher, who had decided the chair could hold him better than his legs. The droplets on his upper lip had become a lake.

"Good grief, Cachita." My mother's eyes darted right and left like a pirate scouring the perfect spot to bury treasure. "How can you be so callous at a time like this?"

"If we had left when I suggested," my grandmother answered, staring at my father, "we wouldn't be in this situation."

He blushed, the same washed out red as my mother's skirt.

I rolled my eyes. This debate was familiar ground.

"I won't leave, nor hold an open house for that jealous band of hyenas, *Mamá*. I'll see them in hell first."

"We're already in it," my grandmother answered. "Just remember your cousin, rotting in that prison hell hole because he distributed flyers criticizing the regime. Or the horrible fate of the Fernandez family."

An unexpected tremor shook my legs. Luis Fernandez had been betrayed by his own brother and executed by firing squad. No one in the community had heard from his wife after she'd been dragged to jail. And as far as Gisela, their daughter—well, I didn't even want to think about her. Forcibly dragged to a work commune in the middle of the Sierra Maestre was not my idea of sacrificing my talents for the revolution, especially when most girls were raped and came back home pregnant and emotionally destroyed for life.

"Must you bring that up, Abue?"

"Yes. You've got to be strong," my grandmother told me, her eyes sad.

"Ramón Fernandez has always been a jealous bastard," my father said of Luis's *chivato* brother. "Never worked for anything, but felt entitled to everything his brother worked for."

"So do most of Castro's hyenas," my grandmother argued. "Only difference is that they're armed. We're not."

My tutor wiped his face with his handkerchief, but clearing his nervous perspiration was a doomed battle. I marveled at the droplets of sweat that now played an incessant connect-the-dot game across his face and neck.

"*Mamá*, this is not the moment to go at each other. We've got to get rid of your stash."

My mother stopped her pacing. With fists pressed against her waist, and legs braced apart, she looked ready to do battle—Wonder Woman with a skirt. "And how do you propose we do that, Emilio?"

"We give it away. As much as possible." My father reached over and grabbed Gustavo. He jerked him off the seat. "Starting with you."

"Forget it," my grandmother said. "I already gave him one box."

My father looked at my tutor, who shook his head like a palm frond buffeted by a strong breeze. Gustavo opened his briefcase a millimeter to show his loot. The familiar red, white, and blue flap of Colgate's FABulous laundry detergent peeked through the gap.

"What about Adela?" my father said.

"She took some last night," my mother answered.

"And gave us a half-used roll of waxed paper," my grandmother added.

My father looked from my mother to my grandmother. "How about Luisa?"

"She didn't need the FAB, but I gave her some canned vegetables for a pound of Valencia rice."

My father flopped on the nearest chair. "The Sagastumes?"

"Got their visas yesterday. They're leaving by week's end. Can't add anything to their inventory—they've already been audited by the *milicianos*."

"How about the Lorenzos, Cachita?" my teacher asked.

"I wouldn't give those *chivatos* the time of day. If the air weren't free, they'd snitch to the nearest *Comité de Barrio* that you were breathing it."

"*Mamá*." My father's fingers furrowed his hair. "Pepe?"

"Exchanged some for powdered milk."

"Benito?"

"His wife is making her own soap."

"Yeya?"

"Gave her half a box in exchange for eggs."

"Until the government takes her chickens," my mother added.

I could see my father turning redder, his blood pressure sky-rocketing with each answer.

"*Carajo*. When did we become a goddamn trading post?" My father pressed his hands into his face. "We're dead."

"What if we put everything in the cistern?" I suggested.

"Flora told me the *milicianos* discovered the Hidalgos using theirs to stash their coffee, rice, and toilet paper," my grandmother said. "Now they inspect every cistern in their searches."

My mother clapped, getting everyone's attention. "I know. Let's dig a hole in the yard, in back of the plantains, and bury the boxes there."

"Might as well place a sign saying: *Search Here*,'" my father said, tapping his forehead with the heel of his palm as though knocking at his brain's door, begging for ideas. "Recently disturbed soil is a dead giveaway."

"What if we pour it down the drains?"

We focused on my grandmother.

"We have four full boxes left," she said. "Let's keep some and pour the rest. The other stuff has its own hiding spots."

I looked at my grandmother with grudging respect. The evidence that could land us in jail would dissolve and wash away into the septic tank. The *milicianos* would come and go without a clue.

"What about the smell?" My father sniffed my mother's recently laundered blouse and hummed in appreciation. He loved clean clothes. "The entire house will stink like a soap factory."

"What if I fry the *croquetas*?" I volunteered. "The cooking will camouflage the smell."

Abue Cachita hugged me. "Brilliant. Simply brilliant. But fry the ones made from that God-awful Russian canned meat."

"Make some coffee, too," my mother told me. "The aroma will divert their attention."

"The free drink and food will distract them more," my grandmother countered.

"Gustavo, you'd better go home," my father said. "If they find you here—"

My mother, more practical, pointed to the front door. "Gustavo, out." She turned to me. "Go upstairs and get ready."

I gathered my book, my pencil, and my notebook, and stuffed everything into the wrinkled paper bag that protected them from the soil in the planter. I lifted the lush fern from its double-boiler-like home, dropped the bag inside, and dumped the plant back in place. With quick strokes, I rearranged the displaced dirt and fronds, then took the terrazzo stairs two at a time.

In my room, I ran to the closet and chose the rattiest skirt I owned. Made of thick linen and dyed black to cover stains and age, the skirt was perfect camouflage for my Bermuda shorts. The blouse that hid my tube top was a favorite of mine—a Safari-styled, khaki, short-sleeved shirt I had used whenever the family had gone hunting ducks with my uncle. I flipped my leather ballerina slippers off my feet and sent them flying into the shady recesses of my closet, grabbed one of the custom-made orthopedic shoes next to my bed, laced it on, and then concentrated on adjusting the metal brace and shoe on my other leg. I hated the contraption—the leather belts, the ones that kept the metal rods in place, made my skin itch. The friction often raised blisters. I couldn't walk without some muscle cramping from the restriction and my knee would hurt after releasing my leg from this unnecessary physical torture.

But a picture of Gisela popped into my mind. *Radio Bemba*, our local rumor mill, had telegraphed the details of the poor girl's fate after she'd been forced to the countryside. Yeya, who had a cousin near the village where Gisela wound up, had given us the gory details to the girl's fate two days ago. As Yeya exchanged some fresh pork from her cousin's small ranch for two cans of condensed milk, some olive oil, and a pillbox of makeup powder from Elizabeth Arden my grandmother had hidden inside the chimney, she recounted the tale of our fourteen-year-old shy neighbor, walking around the village with a belly as round as a ripe watermelon. She'd been gang raped by the very people she'd been forced to alphabetize.

I cinched the leather strap tighter and hobbled my way down the spiral stairs.

In the kitchen, I grabbed a lard cube from the pantry, cut a quarter, and dumped it into a frying pan. As the fat melted, my father's, *I can't believe this*, floated out from the bathroom sandwiched between kitchen and laundry room. His next comment drowned with the flush of the toilet.

I selected eight *croquetas* from the tray in the freezer and heard a gurgle. Another flush. From the laundry room, my mother's complaints competed with the repetitive flushes. "Cachita, this isn't dissolving fast enough."

"Pour more water in," my grandmother coaxed.

Creating a hypotenuse with my restricted leg, I bent to retrieve the cheesecloth cone for the coffee.

"Martica," my father yelled. The porcelain cover rasped against the toilet tank. "Check outside. Anyone coming?" Another flush.

With coffee percolator in hand, I hobbled to the windows over the sink. The street was deserted. The only movement came from the lazy breeze as it combed the fronds of the coconut trees lining our sidewalk.

"No," I yelled back. I packed the coffee grinds against the cheesecloth cone, filled a pot with water, and set it to boil. The lard had finally melted.

"Here, Cachita," I heard my mother say from the laundry room. "Pour half in and place the dirty clothes on top." Hollow clangs followed. From where I stood, the noise sounded like nails rasping and rings banging against the stainless steel drum of the washing machine. My mother and grandmother were probably pushing detergent powder down the holes.

I flicked a drop of water into the liquid lard. Barely a pop. My father whizzed by me, a box of detergent held like a football, a litany of curses floating in his wake.

My grandmother streaked across the kitchen. Two flushes, in rapid sequence, rumbled from the bathrooms upstairs. Abue rushed back with two more boxes of detergent hooked under her arms. She plopped one by the kitchen sink.

"Dump this in the drain when you're done." She went out into the back yard.

Curious, I limped to the open door. Abue was already at our outdoor sink, balancing the laundry tin tub under the faucet. She filled it with some water and stirred in a portion of powder. Before the detergent dissolved, she carefully poured the liquid into the drain. I stared at the small cascade overflowing from the tub's rim, thinking the small flecks of white within the clear water resembled snowflakes etched in moving ice.

"Martica. Where's your brain, *hija?*"

I pivoted, lost my balance, and banged against the doorframe. I bit my inside cheek to prevent cursing out loud.

"How many times have I told you not to leave hot oil unattended?" My mother grabbed two potholders next to the stove and moved the frying pan away from the heat. "The last thing we need is a fire."

"Now, why didn't I think of that?" my grandmother said, patting my head before moving to the kitchen sink. She rose up on her toes, stretched her small frame over the counter as close to the window as possible, and darted a look right and left like a bird searching for bugs. "Burning everything might be the answer to Emilio's concerns."

Water gurgled from the upstairs bathroom as her answer.

"And still land us in jail." Mother stabbed the body of the blue cardboard detergent box on the counter with a butcher knife and carved a long flap across the top. She ripped back the lid and poured an anthill of powder inside the sink.

I placed four *croquetas* in the frying pan, averted my face, and counted to five. Sure enough, the smell of the Russian canned meat invaded the air. I tried not to gag at the overpowering stench of filthy insoles and concentrated on breathing through my mouth, turning the *croquetas* quickly so they would brown faster.

"*Dios,*" my mother said, disgust in her voice. "What on earth do those Russians use for meat?"

"I don't want to know," Abue answered. I saw her fingers busily scraping the overflow of detergent into the drain.

I speared one *croqueta* with a fork and dumped it on the torn piece of grocery paper bag I had spread over a plate to absorb the grease. The *croqueta* hissed and deflated like a soufflé. I fished another from the hot oil and dumped some more to fry. Carefully, I sniffed the air. The stink was bearable. I breathed cautiously.

"Well, I don't care if the *milicianos* eat this batch," I told no one in particular.

I heard the sink faucet spurt out some water.

"At least we don't get food poisoning now that we recognize which cans are bad," my mother said.

My grandmother sniffed louder than the *croquetas* crackling in the hot oil. "We wouldn't be in this predicament if Emilio had listened to me."

I glanced at my grandmother. She poured more detergent down the drain, added water, and pushed everything down with the plunger.

A flush, followed by a clang and a curse, floated down to our level.

"Cachita, if Emilio doesn't fight for our rights from the inside, who will? Besides, everyone is getting fed up with the situation. This won't last."

"Famous last words," my grandmother said and continued scraping at the detergent that now clung stubbornly to the wet enamel of the sink.

Hot oil popped out of the pan and landed on my arm. I jerked, lost my balance, and bumped against the drawer knob. "*Coño*," I whispered, rubbed my thigh, and restored my stability.

"I heard that," my mother said with the keen auditory prowess of Superman.

I returned to my frying, scooping, and dumping the *croquetas* on the brown paper. They kept hissing and deflating, resembling concave cylinders lined up in array form. The boiling water gurgled. I poured it into the coffee, placed our dented tin cup under the cheesecloth, and let gravity do the percolating.

"There," my mother announced triumphantly. A series of soft, hollow pats on the box indicated the last of the detergent. Water poured into the sink, and I heard someone swishing water around. I presumed it was my mother.

A movement to my left caught my eye. My father rushed into the kitchen, only to stop in mid-stride. The smell of these *croquetas* was more powerful than a wall.

"Jesus. Those things stink."

"We could be enjoying real ham *croquetas* if..."

"*Mamá*, enough. I don't..."

"Cachita?"

We all pivoted at once. I was certain my own expression resembled the blind panic my mother's face projected.

"*Coño,* Mirta," my father's voice was as loud as the frying oil. "Don't scare us like that."

Everyone relaxed simultaneously.

Mirta stood framed in the back doorway with two different-sized tin planters nestled within her left arm and two dry coconut seeds cradled in her right. She was a neighbor whose house was one block down from ours. She was a staunch *gusana* and made no bones about denouncing the Castro butchers whenever she could. My father kept saying her outspokenness—and the impressive black market operation of fruits and vegetables she headed—would soon land Mirta in jail. That meant her farmland in Pinar del Rio, owned by her family for more than five generations, would be confiscated by the Castro regime and converted into a *comunidad agraria*—an agrarian community—whose products would be controlled by government minions and used for exclusive consumption by elite *Partido* members, Russian ex-pats, and Canadian tourists.

Not us, the Cuban citizenry.

"What's with the coconuts?" Cachita asked.

Mirta's head pivoted right and left. Satisfied her cursory inspection revealed no unwelcome ears in the vicinity, she placed the planters on the floor. I watched with curiosity. Mirta had taken two tin cans, commonly used by *maniceros* to carry their *cucuruchos* of roasted peanuts around Havana, and had converted them into makeshift flower pots. They made great hiding places. We were using a few to hide my mother's favorite nylon stockings and our family's Café Pilon coffee bags.

"I need help planting these." Mirta's stomach heaved as she straightened. The coconut seeds in her right arm bulged out, as if heaving a sigh.

"Gustavo said you may have a filler to keep the seeds flush with the rim?"

Mirta winked.

Without any prompting, Abue Cachita dove a hand next to the garbage bin, grabbed two folded paper bags from her stash, and snapped one open. A second later, a cascade of snow-colored detergent flakes dropped into the bag's belly, the fresh aroma wafting near me, blocking the smell of the *croquetas* for an instant.

I inhaled, then inhaled once more before the frying food stench could rear up its noxious head to beat the fragrance from the detergent into submission.

My mother recovered from her paralysis.

"Emilio," she ordered. "Go dump the rest of the detergent."

My father stared at the box under his armpit as if it had magically appeared there. He pivoted and rushed into the bathroom.

My grandmother snapped open the other paper bag and repeated the process of filling it with detergent. Meanwhile, my mother scavenged for the aluminum foil box in a kitchen drawer. She collapsed the filled bag onto itself and created a protective covering with the foil. This kept the contents within safe from moisture and dirt while hidden.

A familiar routine in our household.

"What's the latest?" Abue asked.

"I don't know, but something's up. The guard house has been an anthill of activity today."

"Has someone from the *Comité de Barrio* betrayed the Sagastume family?" my grandmother asked, preparing the second bag she had filled so my mother could cover it in foil. "Rolando saw Lidia Lorenzo snooping around their house last night."

"Do you think she saw them smuggling furniture out of the house?" my mother asked. "I know they were planning to give it to family members staying behind."

"I don't know," Mirta said. "I think this is bigger than that. Maybe the rumors of invasion are true?"

My mother made the sign of the cross. "*Ojalá.*"

We were all hoping so, I thought, although we didn't hold much hope since rumors of an invading force had been as constant as the waves crashing ashore with nothing coming out of them. But, yesterday, the newscaster from Radio Free Europe had reported Cuban patriots were launching a counter offensive to wrest control of the island from Castro and his jackals. If this was true, really true, we would be saved from the hell Castro and his sadistic minions had created in our lives.

A motor revved in the distance and a car passed our house. Tires squealed as it took a corner too fast.

I froze. So did everyone else.

Outside, fronds slapped against each other. The coffee dripped into the cup like a leaky faucet. The oil gurgled. My leg itched from the brace straps. Sweat gathered around my upper lip, but I didn't lick it. I only stared at the rectangular patch of world framed by the kitchen window.

It stood empty.

"Do you think..."

"Martica, shush." The order came in four different tonalities, equally urgent.

Silence.

Convinced the wrath of the regime was not falling upon us yet, my mother returned to her task. She gave a final pat to the foil hiding the stash for Mirta, cradled both under her armpit, scooped the tin cans, herded my grandmother and Mirta to the back yard, and got busy.

"If you don't have drainage, they'll get suspicious," I heard my mother say as I caught a glimpse of her arranging small rocks on the inside bottom of one tin can. She reached for the other pot. "Make sure you fill about two inches with soil, Cachita."

My grandmother scooped dirt next to the *guanabana* tree and dumped it inside the pot, then gave it to Mirta, who placed one tin foil submarine inside.

Then the debate began.

I stopped cooking to take a quick glance at these three desperate women, attempting to get the coconut seeds at the right level to prevent detection of the treasure inside.

If this hadn't been so dangerous, it would have been worthy of a *Tres Patines* comedy.

I turned the last batch of *croquetas* and turned off the burner. The action outside was more interesting than finishing my unwelcome task. Besides, the heat from the oil would cook what was left.

Abue Cachita picked up one of the pots. She shook her head.

"It's too heavy." She looked at Mirta. "You'll never get this home in time."

They stood like a Greek chorus, ready to lament the fall of their Cuban Troy. Concentration furrowed their foreheads, their expressions telegraphing a readiness to wail their woes if no solution presented itself.

My mother clapped her hands in satisfaction. "Martica, go get your skates."

"What?" Had I heard correctly?

"Go...get...your...skates."

I limped to the garage as quickly as my brace would allow, retrieved my skates from a storage box next to the doorway, and hobbled back.

I handed the skates over to my mother, who had already unknotted the clothes line there.

My father stopped on his way to another bathroom, saw the women struggling, and slammed the half empty FAB box on top of the counter. "I'll get that."

The women smiled at their knight in shining armor. While my mother held one skate in place, my father balanced the pot on top. My grandmother and Mirta used the clothesline to hold the thing in place. The other flowerpot suffered the same indignities as the first and was latched onto the other like a Siamese twin. Mirta's horde, finally mobile, would be dragged safely home before the searches began.

"*Me voy*," Mirta said in farewell, pushing her hidden cachet. No acknowledgement or thanks was necessary.

I whispered a small prayer for her safety, knowing my family was doing the same.

I returned to the kitchen, realizing I still held onto the fork I had been using to fry the *croquetas*. I limped to the stove and glanced at the frying pan. The *croquetas* I'd left there lay like deflated, burned blimps in a sea of liquid lard. The oil gave a last gasp, burping a bubble, almost as if in final protest at having had to sully its slick surface with the disgusting things.

A horn honked. A car door slammed. Staccato footsteps rushed in our direction, approaching from the garage.

The kitchen clock marked its metronomic rhythm in tandem with my breath, or was it my heart that sounded so loud in my ears? I looked at my parents and my grandmother, wondering if they felt their stomachs cramp like mine. My mother stood like a frozen statue with an empty detergent box pressed against her breasts. The blue box covered her chest like an ancient shield, the bold red letters, blazoned on the cover, standing out like a pseudo coat of arms.

My father's box, on the other hand, lay crushed like an accordion between his hands. Small remnants of white detergent flakes covered his pants and shoes like dandruff, creating a small halo around him.

I stabbed the air with the fork I'd been using. "The boxes," I whispered, horrified. "The boxes."

My grandmother pointed to the frying pan. "The *croquetas*."

My father found the strength to rip his box into little pieces with his bare hands. "Get the garbage pail out."

I scooped the burned *croquetas* and dumped them next to the others. These hadn't deflated as badly as the previous batch.

My mother stabbed her box with a knife from top to bottom in perfectly equidistant dashes, then sawed the box in half. As she ripped, she dropped the pieces on the floor. The debris resembled awkward pieces of a chaotic jigsaw puzzle.

My grandmother, using the kitchen towel as a whip, dispersed the flakes on the floor and on my father's shoes and pants.

I took the garbage pail out and lifted the bag from its home. Stretching down as far as I could with the leg brace, I reached for the ripped cardboard pieces on the floor and dropped everything into the bottom of the pail.

"Not there," my father said, his voice an urgent hiss. "Dump everything under the garbage."

I wasn't going fast enough with the contraption on my leg. Abue Cachita commandeered the garbage bag and plunked the contents on the floor. Plantain peels, squeezed limes with coffee grinds sticking to the inside, chicken bones, broken egg shells, rice grains, and something I didn't quite recognize skittered across the floor.

I turned the pail. The cardboard pieces I'd dropped there plopped out and into the dirty garbage bag my grandmother held open. On hands and knees now, my parents and my grandmother stuffed the garbage strewn on the floor back inside its old home.

A throaty whisper of *Silvia*, heralded with a sense of urgency, reached us.

We all looked at each other. "That doesn't sound like the milicianos," my mother said.

"Sounds like my tutor," I whispered.

A cough and an emphatic clearing of throat was followed by a more desperate, "Emilio."

My father's voice came out as a nervous croak. "Why the hell is he back?"

My tutor appeared and grabbed the back door frame. His chest heaved from the strain of breathing and his face was a pool of sweat.

"The invasion is real," he croaked out. Fear and hope battled for supremacy in his eyes.

Abue Cachita grabbed my father's hand. "Get the radio."

Sweat trickled at the back of my leg, which was getting sorer every time I moved. I excused myself and limped to the bathroom. Inside, I unstrapped the top of the leg brace and sighed in relief.

I heard static and a newscaster's voice: *"Our valiant milicianos, the first line of defense against our imperialist enemies, are bravely confronting the mercenaries that landed in Playa Girón last night..."*

I checked my thigh. The contraption, as usual, had already dug into my skin and the welts were starting to itch and burn. I crossed over to the sink and wet some toilet paper. With slow pats, I cooled down the area around the straps as best I could.

The radio announcer droned on. *"Such patriotism has never been witnessed. The decision to defend, at all cost, the sovereign rights of our country will triumph. We will face the mercenary aggression endorsed and organized by the imperialist Yankees, and we will defeat and crush it with the blood of our martyrs."*

I repeated the cooling method on my thigh and dropped the crumpled paper into the toilet.

"Our glorious Comandante is at the front lines. He will not cower to the enemy that threatens to destroy our glorious revolution."

I flushed the toilet and heard a soft pop. A gurgle.

What was that?

I listened for another second, but the bathroom stood silent. The radio announcer's voice kept rising and falling, a sine curve of enthusiasm and sycophantic idolatry to the revolution. I limped back to the kitchen where things hadn't changed much from when I had left—adults surrounding the radio campfire, their faces lit by hope and fear.

The leg strap branded my skin as I approached. I was no longer faking discomfort. I would be in agony by day's end.

"Traitors to the revolution have been rounded and caged like the animals they are. Schools, stadiums, and prisons are overflowing with these hyenas. But the hammer of revolutionary justice will quash all opposition."

We looked at one another.

"No pity. No quarter. The enemy is surrounded, retreating. Adelante, Cubanos. *March on to victory. The imperialist Yankees are no match for our planes and our resolve. Our revolution will prevail."*

"We're not going to be saved, are we?" Was that rough, choked voice my own?

My mother turned. Her beautiful eyes swam behind a lake of unshed tears.

"No," my father's voice was a whisper of pain.

"Emilio..." My grandmother's voice resonated with a million hopes devoured by an abyss of fatalism. My tutor's thin frame began to shake with the force of his silent weeping.

Defeat marred my father's eyes. "Gustavo. Go home to your family."

My tutor nodded, clapped my father on the shoulder. His retreating footsteps sounded his defeat, a man walking to his doom.

I turned to face the kitchen window, tendrils of agony radiating from my chest. How had such devastation hit our lives? What had we done, as a people, to deserve what this Castro butcher was dishing out? We had lived, had worked, had loved, and had gossiped without hurting anyone. Why such visceral hatred perpetrated against us? But, especially, why wasn't anyone hearing our pleas for help? Why had we been abandoned?

Movement caught my eye. Translucency took on a spherical form, bathed by the wet hand of a rainbow. A bubble seemed to play a floating game with the air. I reached for it. For a moment, the beautiful, glistening sphere hovered over my cupped hand. It rested there for a second, like a whisper, before it popped, leaving my hand empty.

Another bubble puffed up from the kitchen sink. It hung in the air, its surface fluctuating with weeping color.

I marveled at its perfect symmetry before it popped.

And I remembered the detergent.

Suds began to froth from the pipes. More bubbles broke free, levitating into the air without concern, without haste. The septic tank regurgitated its contents, overwhelmed by the sudsy contents we'd rammed into the pipes, sinks, and toilets in our house. In no time, the froth became a wall of foam, overflowing and falling from the sink in defeated clumps around me.

The irony was almost laughable.

But I didn't laugh. I didn't even smile.

My grandmother approached. She stared at the ever-growing suds in silence.

"We should clean this up," I whispered.

Abue Cachita scooped a clump of white foam and studied it for a moment.

"No." She flicked her hand and disposed of the suds like an annoying pest. With her typical determination shining from her eyes, she faced my parents.

"Emilio... I have a plan."

LULLABY

Arrorró mi niño,
Arrorró mi amor,
Arrorró pedazo de mi corazón...
Spanish lullaby

TRAFFIC on US1, like everywhere else in Miami (and practically at all hours now), was similar to driving cattle into a corral: Bumper to bumper mooching and barely any room to maneuver anywhere.

But this was the last passenger drop for Yuniel Roque today. He'd then be free to pick up his son from the day care and have some playtime at Tropical Park before the sun set.

"If you make a left at the next light, you can avoid all this traffic," the woman in the back seat told him. "My house is close-by. I'll guide you."

Yuniel smiled and nodded. Another five minutes of pressing the accelerator and the brakes in tandem, he turned into the side street suggested by his passenger. It was devoid of cars except for the occasional local traffic.

"Make a right at the next light" the woman said. "After that, keep going straight until I tell you."

He nodded once more. Yuniel had been dropping off and picking up customers practically all day from the auto dealer for which he worked, delivering five-star Customer Service to those who dropped their cars for service or for detailing. Whatever the customer wanted, within reason, Yuniel would carry out.

He was proud of his job. He had been named Employee of the Month barely three months into his tenure at the auto dealer. He was efficient, hard-working, respectful, and kept his boss's customers happy. He detailed the company's van every day, replaced the car freshener dutifully every month, and kept mints in a small plastic cup on the dashboard to offer his customers.

Above and beyond service. That was his motto.

And it meant tips, which meant shoes from the Goodwill store for his son. Or a treat of *pastelitos* from the local bakery. He would take anything offered. Even a quarter.

"Thank you for showing me this short cut. This is so much better."

"I know," the woman answered, relieved she'd be home soon. "Traffic is getting like a growing ant's nest. Every day thousands more pour out."

The woman stared at the houses outside the car window for a second. "Do you mind if I ask you a question?"

Yuniel glanced at the woman through the rearview mirror. His smile was his permission.

"You are Yuniel Roque, aren't you? I saw the YouTube of your dramatic arrival in the *Noticiero de las 5* a while back."

His features changed. He didn't like to be reminded of that day. Victory in a sense, loss and defeat in another. He had hated the notoriety. Had been afraid of all the hoopla. In this half-century of Cubans exiled, any triumph that would shove the up-yours to the Fidelista regime was celebrated to the extreme in this town. Yuniel had been the flavor of the week until another *balsero* made it ashore. Yuniel had been grateful for this new darling of the media. The man had launched himself into the Caribbean seven times, only to be returned the same seven times to the Cuban shore where he'd begun his seven odysseys. His eighth attempt, riding the Gulf Stream in an inner tube patched with spit and a prayer, had succeeded, but only after he'd swum for twelve hours straight when his rickety *balsa* floundered. When asked about his blind persistence, he told the reporter he'd wanted to hug the father he hadn't seen since he was four years old, thirty-four years ago.

"Yes," Yuniel answered and hoped that would end the questions.

"I'm glad, you know." The woman's voice was soft.

Yuniel was at a loss.

"I'm glad those boats helped." The woman's face turned into a disapproving mask. "I'm glad they gave you water and pushed your *balsa* until you could get off near Elliot Key. What that Clinton administration did to us from before the days of Elian has been unconscionable."

Everyone knew what had happened before Elian, during Elian, and after Elian. Everyone knew, especially in Cuba, about the changes in the rules of those found drifting in the ocean. Before Clinton had become President, Cubans found at sea could be brought in without reprisal or return. Now, anyone found helping these people, picking them up, or taking them ashore, could face jail time. The only thing the pleasure craft boaters could do, those who found these ocean drifters, was to throw the *balseros* any food and water available before sending them on their way on the same leaking vehicles of death, hoping the drifting sargassum flotsam of Cuban humanity made it to land before the Coast Guard found them. Freedom in the United States now meant feet touching land. If not, they'd be packed back into that Castroist hell hole they'd tried to escape.

"I'm sorry your wife didn't make it."

Yuniel's eyesight blurred. "The boy made it. That's what's important."

"I know." The woman paused, considered. "I know this is rather impertinent, but why did you risk it? Risk him?"

"He would have been of school age next year. His mother didn't want Addiel to go through what we went through in the Cuban school system."

The woman was silent for a moment. Her glance seemed to turn inward, reliving memories of her own.

"I lost a year of schooling myself. My mother had tutors, the few *gusanos* we could find, teaching us until we left the island."

"How long ago was that?" Yuniel asked, curious.

The woman sighed, almost as if in pain. "Too long ago. In the sixties."

Yuniel was silent for a moment.

"The government comes to our houses now and takes the children by force, that is if you don't hand them over when you are expected to. School-age children have to be relinquished to these special centers built in the middle of what used to be sugar cane fields. Once the teachers take charge, the parents are told not to come back."

"What?" The woman was shocked. "I've never heard that."

"No one knows outside of Cuba." Bitterness etched the contours of Yuniel's smile. "I remember when my mother, God rest her soul, left me. I was five. I didn't understand why she'd taken me there, nor why she wasn't allowed to stay, or give me a hug in farewell. When evening fell, and our parents had not returned to pick us up, we were told they had abandoned us. And while we were crying ourselves to sleep, these teachers would come into the bedrooms and tell us that Castro would not abandon us like our parents had. That Castro knew what our parents had done and he was angry with them. *He* would never do what our mothers and fathers had done to us. The teachers soothed all night, pointing to the self-satisfied portrait of the *Comandante*. *He,* they said, would take care of us from now on. *He* would nurture us, feed us, love us. *He* would be our father now, and *he* would make sure we were fed, clothed, and educated." His voice roughened. "And when they finally allowed our parents to visit, they had become resented strangers who'd only given us birth. We were already well on our way to becoming children of the state."

The woman was horrified. "My God. Poor children. Poor Cuba."

"Nelsita didn't want that for her boy. She wanted him to love her, not that butcher Fidel."

The woman didn't answer, but pointed ahead. "Turn left at the corner. My house is the one on the corner, on the right."

Yuniel found the house, parked, and opened the door for the woman to step out. He offered her a candy, but the woman grabbed his hand and squeezed it hard.

"I'm glad you made it with your son. I'm glad he will love you and not that *asesino*, that murderer."

"Mami."

Chubby fingers, not yet slimmed by age, pointed to the woman smiling in the photograph Yuniel held. The four by three picture was wrinkled and stained from exposure to the elements of the Caribbean. But it was a treasure—their treasure. Addiel's mother, Nelsis, had sealed shut this familial memento inside the pocket of the shorts her son had worn the day they had sailed away from

Cuba. It was the only proof that the woman who'd given up her life for the freedom of her child had existed.

"*Y quien es este?* Who's this?" Yuniel pointed to the small boy held in the woman's arms.

The child laughed.

"*Yo.*"

Yuniel squeezed this beautiful boy in his arms. They were on the rocking chair, seesawing gently while finishing their nightly ritual. This little nighttime game, and the gentle swaying to and fro, helped Addiel fall asleep and helped to keep nightmares at bay.

"And where is *Mami?*" Yuniel asked.

"In heaven."

"And she is watching you and taking care of you every day."

Addiel took the photograph and kissed his mom's image.

"Good night, *Mami*. I love you."

Yuniel placed the picture on the empty box he used for a table. The boy settled on his lap, snuggling into position, where his ear could feel and hear the beating of this man's heart.

"*Arrorró mi niño, arroró mi amor, arrorró pedazo, de mi corazón...*"

Yuniel's voice, off key and scratchy, didn't bother the child. It didn't bother Yuniel that he couldn't sing, either. He sang anyway. Addiel's mother had sung this lullaby every night at sea, cradling her boy to sleep in the vastness of the inhospitable ocean. After the boy slept, she would talk to Yuniel about her fears, her dreams for her son, her regrets. And that last day, after the dehydrated and sunburned boy fell into a fitful sleep in her loving, dying arms, she had exerted his pledge.

Promise me, Yuniel. Promise. When I die...

Stop, it, Nelsis. You are not going to die.

When I die, claim him as your son. You don't have any family left in Cuba, and you don't have anyone in Miami, either. Don't let what happened to Elian happen to mine. Addiel can never go back.

Yuniel closed his eyes.

Please, Yuniel. Promise.

He had promised.

And he would keep that promise until the day he died.

ANOTHER DAY IN THE LIFE OF
BENITO JOSÉ FUENTES

"GOOD morning, Mr. Fuentes."

Landon Cooper, customs officer for the great state of Texas, greeted the man who'd been presenting the same papers to him for close to three months. As usual, the rest of the Fuentes family—wife and two daughters—stood behind this soft-spoken man, their expressions expectant and yet despondent.

"Good morning, Mr. Cooper."

Benito José opened the manila envelope in his hands. He retrieved the sky-blue Cuban passports there and passed those over to Cooper. Following a ritual established when he first arrived at the border town of Nuevo Laredo, Benito pulled out the entry papers issued by the US State Department next, as well as the new passport-issue photos and inoculation documents. He pushed those over to Cooper, his eyes as hopeful as his smile.

Landon Cooper checked his files by rote, but he didn't have any encouraging news for these four souls today, either. As he'd done every day for ninety-one consecutive days, Cooper date-stamped the thin strip of paper on his desk, which informed the Fuentes family they would be immediately deported if they set foot on American soil, unstapled the previous one, and clipped the new one to the document.

"Um, Mr. Fuentes." Cooper cleared his throat, uncomfortable with what was coming. "I need you to step aside and wait in that section." He pointed to a separate waiting area to the left. It led to the detention cubicles and an interrogation room.

That was new. Benito José gathered all documentation with meticulous repetition and tried not to worry. He pivoted and opened his arms in a welcoming circle, indicating to his family to gather.

"Mr. Fuentes..."

Benito José paused.

"I'm sorry, Mr. Fuentes," Copper said. "Only you. Your wife and daughters need to wait here."

Cooper turned away from the expression on the man's face. He had never been one to hold fanciful thoughts, but Mr. Fuentes's expression mirrored that of the Atlas of myth, etched in pain, unseen hardship, and blind determination, holding at bay the callous world bearing down on his shoulders.

It didn't seem fair.

Cooper called the next person waiting in line.

Benito gathered his family and guided them to the nearest chairs.

"Benito, what's going on?"

His wife wrung her hands while his eldest, his beautiful Cristina Maria, stared, eyes brimming with tears.

"Are they arresting us?" Amalia Beatriz, his youngest, asked in fear. She crushed her sister's hand, her eyes panicky.

"No, no," he soothed.

"They're sending us back." It was a statement, one his wife had repeated ever since they'd fled Mexico City.

"No, *mi amor.*" Benito led his wife to a chair near the area where he was to wait. For what? "They probably have a few more questions to ask."

"How many more questions do we need to answer? How many more days must we stay in this Mexican border town? I'm afraid, Benito. Really afraid."

Benito pulled his wife into his arms. Elena was almost at her breaking point. So was he. But he must be stronger, stay stronger, for her, for his children.

"It won't be long," he reassured her, although he wasn't so certain things would change soon. "They'll let us through before long."

"And what do we do in the meantime?" Elena asked. "We have to stay in that seedy hotel while you go to work at the nightclub." Elena lowered her voice. "You know what happened the other day when a drunken man almost rammed open the door to our room. And the..."

His wife stopped, glanced at her children. Her next words were barely audible.

"The noises coming from the adjacent rooms were disgusting. Last night, Cristina woke up. She asked what the racket was, but I told her to go back to sleep. I covered her ears."

The eyes his wife turned on him reflected the agony and the humiliation of the moment.

"How can I explain to our children what is going on?" She choked, recovered. "It's nauseating."

Benito's heart hurt. The family had learned quickly what Nuevo Laredo held for them in this year of our Lord nineteen sixty-three. This Mexican town, right across the river from Laredo, Texas, welcomed all American citizens who wanted to escape the dry laws of their state. The no-selling-of-liquor laws were manna to this side of the border where, every weekend, hordes of young men and women crossed the Rio Grande, mingled with the locals, partied, patronized night clubs, drank hard liquor, and fornicated all night long. Businesses encouraged the crossover. Sales were brisk for all the local merchants, including their hotel. Benito suspected it served as a *tumbadero,* a cathouse, for the weekend.

If he had been alone, it wouldn't have been so bad. He worked busing tables and cleaning the nightclub until the wee hours of the morning. But his wife couldn't work, staying with the girls all day, and dreading the nights. To make matters worse, the room they rented had thin walls and a wide, open rectangle near the ceiling that connected their room to the adjoining one. You could hear anything and everything. A drunken man had even used the opening as target practice once, throwing squashed beer cans through the opening, laughing uproariously after scoring a hit-through.

Elena and the girls had been terrified, huddled on the opposite corner of the room, while beer cans, some with beer in them, fell near their bed and splashed the remaining contents on the dingy floor. For days, the room had reeked of rancid alcohol.

But Benito was powerless to do anything at the moment. That hotel room was all they could afford.

"I'll ask my coworkers to see if they know of another decent place to stay."

But he doubted that existed. Their part of town was better than the other end of town. He could not expose his family to worse hazards.

"Mr. Fuentes?"

Benito turned. Two men, almost identical in their black suits, thin black ties, white shirts and crew cuts, stood side by side, watching him. The blonde one held a file. The other one watched.

"Yes?"

"Please come with us."

Elena crushed his hand. "Benito?"

"Everything will be fine. I'll be fine."

Cristina began to cry. "*Papi.*"

Amalia Maria glued herself to his waist, her small frame trembling against him.

"Elena, Cristina." He opened his arms and embraced them all. He stroked Amalia Maria's soft hair, comforting her as he had soothed her since she'd been born.

"Shh, *mi niñita linda.* Everything will be fine." He hugged his wife and other child in turn. "Don't worry. I'll be fine."

He kissed his wife's cheek. "Wait for me." He took out a precious dollar bill, one that needed to be saved. "Buy the kids a soda, some snacks. I'll come back soon."

Benito approached the men, who turned without waiting for him to draw near. They led him through a few hallways, until they reached a small interrogation room.

"Please have a seat," the blonde man pointed to the chair across from where he stood.

Benito faced the man who seemed to be the one in charge. He looked military, not immigration. What could this be about?

Before Benito could open his manila folder, the man stopped him.

"We don't need to see your papers, Mr. Fuentes. You're here to answer our questions."

"I don't understand. Aren't our papers in order?"

"State Department issues many documents, Mr. Fuentes, but we're Justice. If we don't give the okay, your entry papers are worthless." The man opened the file. "And we have issues with your application. You'll have to satisfy us before we allow you to enter...*if* we allow you to enter."

Benito was shocked. Had they made a mistake in seeking asylum in the United States? President Kennedy had assured all Cubans desiring freedom from the anvil of communism that they had a place in America. It was the only country where they could live at the same economic, cultural, and political level they'd had when living in Cuba. They were poor now, but he planned to reach his goal of living as well as they'd had in Cuba. It would take several years of sacrifice, revalidating his medical license, using whatever support group other exiles in the same position offered. There was so much they'd given up already, so many humiliations suffered, so many things lost. And there would be many more before they made it.

"You stated in your application that you did not belong to the Communist Party."

"I don't..."

The man picked the top paper, turned it, and slid it slowly across the table. His forefinger drummed a section of the document copy.

"This," he tapped, "says you do."

Benito stared at the Xerox copy of a Medical Doctors Association membership. He saw his name written in a beautiful scripted hand. A small box was checked in the corner. That had been added after nineteen sixty-one by a government that wanted to control all professionals. You don't sign up, you don't belong. You don't belong, you don't work. Many, not realizing the brutality of the new government, had refused to sign on principle. Government agents had then breached their homes, beaten them unconscious, and thrown them in jail. Only the government knew what else happened to those poor souls. The rumor was many had been *fusilados*, shot to death in the Cuban *paredones*. So, if you wanted to work in the island, at least earn a meager and ever decreasing wage, every member of a professional society not only had to say they belonged to the Communist party, but had to renew their commitment yearly.

But his active status had been rescinded a year ago when it had become clear he would be of no use to the Castro regime.

"I'm not a communist," Benito argued softly. "But if you wanted to work... No. If you wanted to survive, you had to check that box. You have to understand..."

The blonde man held up a hand. "We understand perfectly. And you are lying. You are probably another Commie infiltrator."

Benito's hackles rose, his anger simmered.

"Do not compare me to those murderers," Benito almost shouted, but remembered where he was, and whom he was facing. He'd faced worse interrogators for over a year. He needed to settle, for his family's sake.

"I am a preeminent cardiac surgeon..."

"You, sir, are nothing until you certify to a US Medical Board that you are even qualified to hold a knife in your hand."

Benito stared, at first insulted and then, deflated. They were right. He and his family were nothing. They'd lost, leaving reputation, status, family, generations of history, and their very identity in the Cuban dust. He, his wife, and his children would have to rebuild everything, even their souls, from nothing.

"You were in the Soviet Union for three months last July," the man continued his interrogation. "Why were you there?"

Benito answered, his voice deflated, as if in surrender. "The government shipped us there to share with Russian doctors the latest methods in cardiac surgery."

"Why didn't you refuse if you aren't part of the system?"

"Are you serious?" Benito couldn't believe these men had no clue. "You have no choices in Cuba. You either went, or you and your family would be jailed. And, have you seen the conditions of Soviet hospitals? They are mired in nineteenth century mentality, with barely any technological advancement. We had to teach them, not the other way around."

The man didn't comment. He read more notes written in the file.

"You claim you want to enter the United States for political reasons. Are you sure they are political and not medical?"

"My Cuban visa to Mexico expired a month ago. If Castro's minions find me, I'll be taken back, and I will never see the light of day. My life, my family's life, will be forfeit."

"Mr. Fuentes," the man said, leaning back in his chair, steepled fingers in front of his chest. "We are a country of laws. If you swear, like you did, that the information given in this application for entry into the United States is the truth, the whole truth, and nothing but the truth, I could consider you for entry. But you have lied about being a communist, and now you are lying about your reasons for asylum. You're here for medical issues. I can't really allow you to take advantage of our citizens' charitable souls and their taxes."

"I'm not sick."

"You have Parkinson's, sir. You are dying."

Benito sighed. He knew this would be coming.

"No, I don't. I have been faking the symptoms for over a year."

The man stared at Benito, half-surprised, half-skeptical.

"After my colleagues and I were sent to the Soviet Union," Benito began. "I realized what was in store for our country, how Castro would subjugate the Cubans, and what extremes our government would take in order to maintain power. My beautiful Cuba would be destroyed. So would we.

"But, to a certain extent, I was still one of the lucky ones. My skills were precious to the government. Doctors, together with ballet dancers, baseball players, and other scientists were the sacred cows of the Castro regime. He planned to use us as his personal envoys, his worldwide propaganda mouthpieces perpetuating the myth his revolution was utopia on earth. I took advantage of this privilege, and I came to a decision."

"And what was that?" the man asked.

"I faked Parkinson's. Castro has no use for sick people, let alone dying doctors who cannot be cured, you see. I had no son, just two daughters, so they were worthless to the regime."

"You expect me to believe this?"

Benito shrugged. "You may or not, but I'm willing to be examined by your doctors. They will see I'm not lying."

For the first time, the other man spoke.

"How did you pull it off?"

Benito closed his eyes, concentrated. Bit by bit, he transformed. First the shaking of fingers, head, arms. He reached for the file with an awkward slowness. He stood. His torso became rigid and, added to the loss of balance, he exaggerated postural instability.

Within another minute, he was back to his regular self.

"I am a doctor, gentlemen," he said. "I know the symptoms, how they set on, when. It is the only disease that cannot be diagnosed with a blood test or an X-ray, so my deception could not be discovered. If I messed up, my life would be over. I told no one, not even my wife. It took me a year to make sure other doctors saw evidence of the neurological markers of the disease, how it progressed, until a unanimous diagnosis was given. Only then did I seek medical treatment outside of Cuba."

"You were allowed to leave?"

"As a sick man I'm useless to Castro and his cronies. I asked for a medical visa, knowing they would give one. I was to be treated by a colleague in Mexico. I never went to him. As soon as we arrived, I reached out to a colleague in UNC, Dr. Bridgewater, who helped get my documentation processed and in order. Now, I'm on the lamb, as you say, from the Cuban government. We are in jeopardy of being caught and sent back. The repercussions of what I did would be unspeakable."

The men stared at one another. The blonde man gathered the loose papers and stood. So did the other man.

"Thank you, Mr. Fuentes. We'll contact Dr. Bridgewater, review your file further. We'll let you know what our decision will be."

Benito stood. He shook hand with both men, not out of courtesy, but to show them his grip was strong, without twitches.

As he walked back to his wife, Benito thought about the obstacles he'd overcome to arrive here. It would be ironic indeed if what he had done in order to leave the yoke of communism would be the very thing that would seal his family's fate.

He refused to think of the alternatives.

Landon Cooper, Immigration Officer for the great state of Texas, looked around the room for the familiar face he'd greeted for close to three months. But the countenance of his Atlas was nowhere to be found.

As he checked a Mexican passport and stamped it, Cooper wondered if Mr. Fuentes was ill. Could he have overslept? He hoped so. In the back of his mind, a nagging fear knocked. He hoped Mr. Fuentes and his family wouldn't take the route of others in his position. Cooper liked this family. Felt for them. He would hate for them to become wetbacks, especially because of what had happened yesterday. The repercussions, jail and deportation when caught, would be awful.

And these poor exiles didn't deserve it.

Cooper called for the next person in line and glanced at the two men waiting for Mr. Fuentes. They'd been waiting for an hour. If they realized the Fuentes's were a no-show...

Cooper kept checking and stamping.

The agents from Justice fidgeted, glanced at their wristwatches.

Cooper stamped another passport. He handed it back to the woman, searched beyond her, and smiled. There they were, patient in their distress, at the end of the line. He told the next man to wait and waved for the Fuentes family to step forward.

"Good morning, Mr. Fuentes," he said. "I am very happy to see you here today."

"Good morning, Mr. Cooper," Benito answered. "Glad to be here. Sorry we're late."

As he had been doing for over three months, Benito José opened the manila envelope in his hands. He retrieved the sky-blue Cuban passports there and passed those over to Cooper. He pulled out, as well, the entry papers issued by the US State Department next, together with the new passport-issue photos and inoculation documents. He pushed those over to Cooper, his eyes as hopeful as his smile.

"Sorry I don't have the answer you seek today, either, Mr. Fuentes."

Benito stared at this man who, from the beginning, had been courteous and friendly.

"There is always hope, Mr. Cooper. Things will change, eventually."

Cooper unstapled the strip he'd placed there yesterday. He date stamped the new one and placed the slip inside the passport.

Benito, with a restraint born of desperation, collected all the documentation and placed it neatly inside the manila envelope. He gathered his family in a hug, kissed his wife, and walked to the two men from the Justice Department for further questioning.

This time, however, he felt he walked to a hopeful future.

Another day. Another chance.

He smiled.

PROLOGUES

INTO THE LIGHT

"MAGDA, please."

Magda Evans, curator of the *Museum of the Weird, the Sad, and the Wretched* waved a dismissive hand in the air.

"They'll be here any minute. Is everything ready?"

"Will you please listen to me?"

"Katherine, I don't have time for your mumbo-jumbo nonsense."

"But, Magda..."

"No, no, and no."

Katherine Gates, friend, employee, and over-all administrator of Magda's delirium (as Katherine called the museum), rushed after the woman who was a cross between a down-to-earth Katherine Hepburn and an elegant Grace Kelly. A true dynamo of 70 summers, Magda was a whirlwind of energy and enthusiasm, whose interest in weird local history had become a true vocation. She'd taken the old train depot building in their small town, restored and turned it into a museum that served as a visitors' information center for the historic downtown.

Unfortunately, that wasn't the problem here. The most frustrating issue now was that Magda believed her museum was haunted; and she was on a mission to prove it.

"This is insane," Katherine said, but what she really wanted to do was wail. Her friend had no idea what she could unleash. What she had already cracked open.

"You've had three crews, in what, seven months, and they've gotten zilch? What makes you think this one will?"

"They are the best, according to my sources," Magda replied.

"Bunk. These so-called experts are nothing of the sort. And all the so-called evidence is bogus."

Magda stopped in mid-stride and twirled to face her.

"Don't you tell me, young lady, that you haven't heard the tap-tapping from that Royal typewriter found in Antarctica, frozen fingers of the typist still attached to its keys."

"Really..."

"Or seen that shadow on the security tape near the memento mori I acquired a month ago."

"Magda," Katherine said, her patience at the limit. "That tap-tap, as you call it, was the pipes expanding with the heat. And the shadow was a bug on the lens."

"Matter of opinion." Magda pivoted and walked with brisk steps toward the front door.

That woman is delusional.

Katherine jerked. Why was it Jacob always came at the most inopportune moments?

Jacob...Not...Now.

Your friend has no idea what she's playing with, Kat.

Katherine agreed with him. This new obsession of Magda's was dangerous. But like everyone else who delved in these ghost hunts, people truly didn't understand the reality of what they were really bringing into the light. One thing was to guess, speculate, and theorize, another was to know.

And Katherine knew.

"Ah, here they are." Magda stood at the open doorway, like a Hollywood grande dame welcoming her guests.

The van from the reality show *Paranormal Revealed* parked near the handicap ramp. Host and crew disgorged from it like ants from an anthill, but one man in particular approached. Magda hummed.

"Now that is what you call eye candy," she whispered. "Wish I were thirty years younger to romp with this Alpha."

Katherine watched, curious. She had been on vacation when Magda had had the initial interview with the show's producer, Cris

Ocampo. A quick up-down inventory of the man and she had to agree with her friend. He was a drool fest. Tall (what? Six, six-one?), with muscles sculpted by serious weight training that stood shy of being overly bulky. Brown hair, longish on top, gel-molded backward. Angular face framed by thick brown brows, and a megawatt, orthodontic-perfect smile that lifted his prominent cheekbones. Oval eyes, a light milk-chocolate in color, gloriously outlined by long, dark chocolate lashes she'd sell her house to have. And the expression in those eyes made her stomach flip. Sad eyes, she called them, not sure if the expression (and the impression they made on her) was due to their shape, or the presentiment secrets huddled below their surface. This man, Katherine thought, had seen a few things in life and experienced much more than most.

They also reminded her of Jacob's eyes somehow.

Magda leaned in, conspiratorial, and whispered from the corner of her mouth. "Take note, sweetie. He's single, smart, and rich."

Katherine narrowed her eyes when she saw the familiar, I'm-going-to-get-you-a-man look on her friend's face.

"O.M.G." Her whisper was hoarse and angry. "You didn't."

"Of course not. But it doesn't hurt to expose you to what's out there."

"For God's sake, when are you going to stop matching me with every male who walks through the front door?"

Magda's expression softened. "You need to get out of your shy shell. You deserve to be happy."

"I am happy."

"No. You are lonely. And you are always alone."

She's correct, you know.

Please be quiet. We have a problem here.

"Miss Evans?" Ocampo asked.

Magda purred some more.

The man's voice played harmony with Katherine's insides.

Good grief.

"Magda, sweetie. Just Magda." She extended her hand and pulled Katherine to her side. "This is Katherine Gates, my assistant, confidante, and friend. She'll stay with you tonight in case you need anything." She gestured for him to follow.

Mega-watt smile upped the wattage. He reached back and pulled the host of the show forward.

"And this is the host of our show, David Zunich."

David Zunich, best known for his television persona of Forteus, was a bit emaciated. Dressed and made up very Emo, he added detail to his character with greasy ebony hair, which covered one of his black kohl, highlit eyes. Tattoos of spiritual reference on arms and neck completed the stereotype. To Katherine, he resembled a cross between Marilyn Manson and Criss Angel. Very freaky supernatural.

"Thank you again for inviting us, Magda," David said. "You have a very unique place here."

Magda loved any praise of her museum. "Great bones. Just needed a facelift and tender loving care."

David, hands on hips, did a three-sixty in place, as though gauging lighting, acoustics, camera angles, and overall atmosphere of the place.

"I also see what you meant, Magda. I can feel something...a heaviness, if you want to know. "

Magda preened.

Katherine and Cris huffed at the same time.

Sad eyes focused on her, speculation in them.

Oh crap.

The patterns of the warped floorboards suddenly fascinated her. The least she wanted was for someone to be aware of her tonight.

"Where would you like to set up, Cris?" Magda asked.

Katherine sighed in relief at her friend's distraction.

"Nowhere special. As a matter of fact, it would be more natural to let our cameras roll as you're walking around with David. As he interviews you for this segment, we'll tape everything, including the rooms of interest. That will give our viewers background information about the museum, the pieces here, and what psychical phenomena they might trigger. We'll edit, once we are back at the studio, and add explanatory voice-overs where needed."

"Fabulous. When will you start?"

"As soon as we get the equipment set up."

Katherine locked the front door of the museum and tried to calm herself. Magda had left an hour ago. Cameras, video equipment, cables, and crew were all set up and ready to go green on the producer's order. Everyone was excited, geared up to catch evidence of the supernatural and show it to the world. But the next few hours or so would be nightmarish for Katherine. She breathed long and deep, exhaling it in a soft whisper. She needed strength for what was coming. She needed to get ready for battle.

She rested her forehead on the cold door surface and closed her eyes.

St. Michael, St. Gabriel, St. Raphael, assist us with your angels. Help us and pray for us.

She turned her head slightly. Jacob stood a few paces away on her left, his expression one of patient suffering, one of solemn sorrow.

He, like her, knew the struggle to come.

She smiled in encouragement. Jacob was a Poor Soul, her Poor Soul, one of the neglected ones at the lowest level of Purgatory. He'd appeared to her last year, God only knew why, and had stayed. Katherine believed the moment of attachment had occurred during her last vacation in Spain—inside the nave of a twelfth century, Norman-Romanesque church in the area of A Coruña, if she were exact. She recalled that, as she had walked around, fascinated by the architecture, she'd been drawn to a small recess near the altar. There, cut into the wall, a sepulcher with a stone effigy in the image of a medieval warrior caught her eye. And, as she was reading the small plaque with Jacob's name on it, an overwhelming sadness shook her. Not a normal human sadness, but one the souls felt as they waited for liberation. On impulse, she'd posed her hand on the rough stone image and, like she had been doing since she was fifteen years old, whispered...

...have mercy on those who are completely forgotten...

Promised a Mass...

...deliver him from his pain...

And offered her prayer...

...grant this man eternal peace.

Jacob had appeared in her living room a week later, at first silent, then selectively talkative, but never revealing what he needed from her. Prayers and Masses had been offered, but there was one particular action needed, one that had not been revealed even to him.

Not even his Guardian Angel, who shared in his suffering in Purgatory, knew.

And it was frustrating as heck for her.

She turned around and watched as Cris Ocampo gave last minute instructions to the crew monitoring the static IR cameras.

He doesn't believe.

I don't know about that, Jacob.

Let me clarify. He doesn't believe this Forteus has any supernatural gift or captures anything remotely supernatural.

Anybody can see that.

Jacob looked at her. *You are special, you know.*

Yeah. Right. She felt the cold gather, encroach. The shadows were assembling.

We are ready, Jacob told her.

Katherine started to nod, but stopped when she realized Cris Ocampo watched her. It was a bit unnerving the manner in which he scrutinized her, almost as if he were dissecting her every move, expression, and mannerism.

Time to hide where they'd told her to sit while filming. She'd be out of the way, unseen in her corner. And she wanted to remain unseen. She preferred...no, scrap that. She sought anonymity and silence, wrapping around herself a bubble of prayer, her actions secluded and only open to the eyes of God.

With her left hand inside the baggy sweatpants' pocket, she squeezed the rosary she'd placed there, and walked to the chair set far behind the crew's Command Area.

I believe in God...

Cris Ocampo did a cursory check of crew, equipment, and cast. Everyone was in autopilot now. All lights had been extinguished a while ago, and David, together with his two sidekicks, roamed the train depot turned museum, their voices echoing and ethereal in the darkness.

For close to six years, he had been the producer of this show. For six years, he had made sure this cash cow of a program remained fresh and entertaining. For six years, cast and crew had wandered across the nation catching ambiguous noises, EVPs that could be interpreted as anything by anyone. They'd taped shadows, with David's enthusiastic voice-over explaining the blacker voids captured. But Cris knew better. These so-called shadows were really figments created more by suggestible minds rather than actual manifestations filmed.

And after six years of the same, Cris was bored to tears at the nonsense, not to mention the effort it took not to laugh at the idiocy from the cast members in their belief they had any impact on the paranormal, let alone that they could command the appearance of spirits at a whim.

"This is Forteus, Keith, and Luca from the Paranormal Revealed *crew..."*

Cris believed there were unexplainable things in this world. What he didn't believe was that the spiritual performed at the ready command of the living, as his cast and crew believed.

"We're here at the Museum of the Weird, the Sad, and the Wretched *where paranormal activity has been witnessed. According to the owner, Magda Evans, these paranormal manifestations began a year ago, right after renovations on the old rail station ended..."*

Tonight, however, something was off. Cris felt it. And it had to do with the striking woman who had remained with them at Magda's order. Beautiful, in an earthy way. Shy, gauging from some of her reactions. Incisive eyes, malty beer in color, pinched nose, and kissable soft lips. But that wasn't what was throwing him off. Typically, patrons and their assistants were necessary pests. They wanted in on every detail about the taping of the show. Oftentimes, those same people stood in the way, star struck, bobbing heads and agreeing with everything said and experienced, regardless if events were false. And always, everything David suggested was taken as gospel, whether it was a word caught on an EVP, or a floating light orb captured on tape, or a word flashing across an Ovilus III spirit box.

Useful idiots, all of them.

Then there was Katherine Gates.

"Magda and her employees have experienced strange psychic events, and she is afraid for her employees' safety..."

A choked snicker came from the direction where Katherine Gates sat, a dark shadow within the darker shadows of the room.

"This Mel meter will register any fluctuations in temperature and electromagnetic pulses anywhere in the building where spirit activity is present."

Magda's assistant was a true enigma. She had not fawned, mingled, or asked a single question during set up. When she'd locked them inside the museum earlier, she'd stayed by the door as if in deep prayer. If he had not been aware of her every move, he would have missed the slight tilt of her head and the slight nod of acknowledgement, cut off the instant she'd become aware he was watching. And as she had waited for the lights off order, and for the taping to begin, Katherine had been a silent statue standing in a forgotten corner.

"We already set up our static, night vision cameras, and have set REM pods in the two rooms where paranormal activity has been witnessed. We'll also use some of the museum objects to trigger responses from any spirits who are close."

Cris rubbed his eyes and turned back to the night vision camera on which he kept watch, not on the cast of the show, but on this enigmatic woman.

"The question, though, is this: is this place really haunted? That's our purpose here tonight. We will reveal to you anything from the spiritual realm we can gather, or debunk what appears to be spiritual, but that is really normal and explainable."

Cris narrowed his eyes. There. There it was again, that lightning flash of humor, that slight lifting of her lips in a polite smirk. Or was that another snicker? What was going on in the mind of this fascinating woman?

"Luca, you have the thermal?"

His intuition warned something was up this evening, and that he'd be witness to it.

"Ready and working."

And it revolved around Katherine Gates. Meanwhile, she sat, waiting.

Waiting for what?

That was the puzzle he had to decipher tonight.

Curiouser and curiouser.

He's watching.

Can't help that, Jacob.

Ocampo is different. Senses something. He's aware, unlike anyone here tonight.

Maybe. But we have a bigger problem tonight.

Its tendrils are out, but it's keeping its distance. The frustration grows stronger, so it'll slam hard. Are you going to be okay?

Do I have a choice?

You do.

Yeah, but I'm not going to let this one through. I just can't believe Magda opened the way for it. If I hadn't been sick that day...

It would have found another way through.

But why, Jacob? Why only this one entity over and over? Most of the time it's Poor Souls that come through, needing prayers and Masses. Anything else, well, you know what they are.

The dark ones deceiving, creating chaos and turning those they can down the wrong path, the wrong understanding.

This one is different, as though it has an agenda and has been granted permission to pursue it.

You're afraid this thing is targeting you?

Not me. Us, Jacob. Us.

The purpose behind this remains veiled to my sight. I can't see beyond to understand.

Well, let's concentrate on the now. I hope these idiots don't do something stupid tonight.

If they stay true to their model, the protective circle of souls should be strong enough to keep everything at bay.

"Let's start with an EVP session here," David's voice, clear and strong, broke through the darkness. "Magda said she's heard tapping sounds coming from this typewriter here."

Stay strong, Kat.

"Is anyone here with us?" David asked, and tapped a few keys.

The cold that had been a nagging reminder on her skin seeped deeper, snaking through muscle fiber until her extremities iced over. She felt the Poor Souls converge tighter, the light emanating from their Guardian Angels a kaleidoscope of pixie dust.

"What's your name?" David continued. "Did you use this typewriter to express your last wishes? To confess your sins?"

A small noise in the distance, like a pebble falling.

"What was that?" David's voice held an edge of excited fear. "Stop. Everyone stop. Did you hear that?"

Silence.

"Let's see if we captured that on tape."

Katherine glanced at the director's monitor several feet in front of her without stopping the litany of prayers in her mind. The three men huddled over the recorder. She heard David's voice repeating his previous words. The small noise.

The darkness on her right bulged.

She pushed back with more prayers.

Retaliation came in pinpricks, sharp and hot.

Her muscles protested. The back of her neck became a conduit for electric currents, scraping her skin and raising a panicky flight instinct in her body. She tamped it down. Her fingers spasmed on her rosary.

Our Father, who art in heaven...

Outside the circle of protection, shadows roiled. Katherine heard their cries of despair, of hate, screams for a deliverance that would never come.

The sounds of hell.

The screeching of the REM pod in the main room filled the air.

Katherine flinched at the noise, breathed in through her mouth. Her bones burned now. This must be how spontaneous human combustion felt.

"Did you catch that, Mike?" David asked.

Mike, the director monitoring all cameras at Command Center, spoke into the walkie-talkie.

"Yeah, we caught that on tape. But I think it was a moth passing near the antenna. I saw something flutter on screen. I'll check."

While Mike verified, Katherine saw David and his cohorts walk around the main room, close to her desk.

"Are you here with us? Come talk to us. Use our energy. If you speak into this recorder in my hand, we'll be able to hear you."

Holy Spirit...deliver us from evil.

A walkie-talkie chirped. "Debunked. A moth," Mike told David.

Things settled. The circle of protective souls stayed strong, repudiating anything wanting to toy with these people, confuse them.

Katherine was grateful her soul helpers were keeping the others at bay. But she wasn't fooled. The dangerous one was near. Waiting.

An hour passed. Then another. And because nothing was happening, David and his co-hosts got increasingly frustrated. They took the silence as a personal affront.

"Are you playing with us?" David's voice echoed. "Is that what is happening?"

No, no. Shut up, stupid. Don't provoke.

Kat, concentrate.

She felt the circle shift, rearrange. Jacob appeared beside her and squeezed her shoulder.

The connection angered the darkness.

To her left, blackness congealed into a Stygian form that obliterated all light. Hopelessness assailed her emotions. Vindictiveness. Visceral loathing. Katherine drowned in darkness, despite her prayers. Pain speared her, consumed her. She panted, her facial muscles etched in pain.

The thing was near. Too close. Too close.

"I think you are here," David shouted, taunting. "But you're a coward. Show yourself."

Oh, God. Oh, God. Stop, you idiot. Shut. Up.

Katherine curled into an armadillo pose. The blackness expanded.

Jacob tensed.

A whisper slithered across her hearing. Laughter, low, malicious, a penetrating snigger rumbling from the bowels of the very earth.

It was here. And it knew this Forteus could finally set it free.

If David's next words were what she suspected, they would unleash what she'd been desperately trying to bottle up. And if the genie escaped from its bottle...

A strong hand covered her own, its hold powerful, almost strangling in its intensity.

"Are you all right?"

The darkness retreated. She didn't understand.

He brings light. Hold on to it.

Katherine's eyes fastened on the man who'd been studying her all evening. Was that horrified concern mirrored there? Or was she hallucinating?

Katherine shook her head, unable to utter a sound.

Tell him. Use him. He can help stop this.

Katherine nodded. Accepted.

"What's wrong?" Cris's voice was more a demand than a question.

The creature ripped at her in backlash.

"Stop him," she whispered.

Cris leaned forward, his lips close to her ear. "You mean David?"

A symbiosis flashed between them, seemed to overcome her. What the hell? Katherine knew Cris had felt it, too.

"Yes," she panted. "He must not order this thing through. He mustn't."

"You can't play with us," David said, his voice reverberating with righteous indignation. "You can't hide from me, you asshole."

Her hand convulsed. "Stop him."

Cris stared at her for a second.

"I'm through playing your game," David shouted. "I command..."

Cris threw his camera on the floor. It skittered over the floorboards and stopped by the feet of his astonished crew.

The noise, and Cris's colorful, loud cursing, froze everyone in place.

"Well, this was a damn bust," David said.

He looked tired, so unlike the energetic enthusiasm he'd brought when arriving at the museum hours ago. Things had not panned out the way he'd expected, especially after the camera incident. The chaos that ensued had lasted but for a moment. In the wake of apologies and resets, they'd all gone back to work. Unfortunately for Forteus and friends, the EMF meters had remained stubbornly unlit, REM pods had stayed silent, and FLIR cameras had had no thermal hits or fluctuations.

No EVPs. No orbs. No shadows.

A few bumps in the night, easily debunked.

Otherwise, a complete dud.

Except for THE incident.

And only two people knew the truth behind it. Well, she knew the complete truth. Cris suspected the rest. But both of them were keeping mum.

"Ms. Evans will be disappointed that there is nothing paranormal here," Katherine said, exhausted, wanting them out of the museum and out of her life. "She greatly admires your work."

"Well, these things happen occasionally," David said, stepping out into the cool dawn. Cris, however, remained by Katherine's side, not budging an inch.

"Spirits don't always manifest, you know," David continued. "And even if this was an off night, that doesn't mean the museum is not haunted. Thanks for inviting us, though. The place is really cool. And Magda can call us if the activity persists."

"I'll relay your message. Thank you for all your help."

"Why don't you wait for me in the van, David." Cris sent him on his way with a slight push. "I need to wrap up a few thing with Ms. Gates."

David shook hands with her and walked away.

Cris didn't waste a second. He caught Katherine's hand and pulled her back into the room. He clearly wanted to maintain any conversation private.

"Here." He grabbed the chair behind the desk and rolled it near her. "Sit. You're about to keel over, you look that tired."

Katherine sat, grateful.

"Talk to me."

The man looked intense. Worried. He probably wouldn't put up with any bull from her, either. Katherine knew if she didn't satisfy his questions, Cris Ocampo would haunt her until he received the answers he needed.

Should she trust? She'd been at this for so long. So alone.

Cris knelt and pulled her hands into his. He stroked them, his touch soothing, comforting.

"What the hell was going on here last night? What was that *thing?*"

Interesting, Kat. He not only felt, he saw.

"Are you sure you want to know?" Katherine asked softly.

"Hell, yes. That sucker was a solid mass of blackness, but when I tried to push through to reach you, my hand went through it like touching air. I've never seen anything like it."

"Neither have we. But the entity has been trying to come into the light ever since Magda decided to have a Ouija board séance here."

"That was intense, Katherine. And don't give me any bull. You were attacked. You were in pain. What the hell were you trying to do?"

Kindly tell him to stop using the word hell. Not seemly. Not after tonight.

Katherine smiled.

"Damn, but you're doing it again."

"What?" She was confused.

"The nodding, the listening, the smirking, as if you're having a private conversation with a spirit."

Advise this human I'm no mere spirit. That's insulting. I'm a Poor Soul.

"His name is Jacob, and he is a Poor Soul attached to me."

Cris did a double take. "You mean a soul, like in Purgatory soul? That's insane."

Katherine cocked her head, studying him, curious. "You're the producer of a paranormal show, yet you're questioning this?"

Cris released her. He paced his frustration.

"I believe there are spirits around us. Some stay, some go. I've felt things I can't quite understand. But Purgatory?"

"It's difficult, isn't it? A reckoning exists, and that blows our minds. The reason why we fear death, I think. It's so much easier to believe in a Kumbaya theory where we'll simply cross into the light, despite our sins, and live happily ever after."

"Can't believe this."

He believes.

"Well, I can't help that."

"You said that thing last night wants to materialize?"

"It almost did last night."

"What stopped it?"

"Prayer. The Poor Souls and their Guardian Angels creating a cordon of protection. My suffering in exchange for safeguarding the living."

And so much more we didn't have the time to tap.

Katherine ignored Jacob.

"You helped, too."

"Yeah, right. Destroying expensive equipment so that the host of my show would shut up."

"Summoning is dangerous business. Provoking is worse. You brought..." Katherine paused, tried to explain. "A light. An energy, if you will. By touching me, helping me, you added strength to the circle. The entity was not happy being sucked back into the darkness."

Cris visibly shuddered. "Do you know what it was?"

"A demon, probably." She paused. "Maybe."

It could be a condemned soul.

Katherine didn't want to consider Jacob's words.

"This is incredible." Cris eyes shone. "You have an incredible gift."

"No, Cris."

"What?"

"No. No one must know what happened here, what I do. And if you ever reveal it, I'll ridicule you as someone whose sanity just flew the coop."

Cris stared.

"I'll lie through my teeth until the universe ends and calls you a liar."

"Why? Others would love..."

"I'm not them. This is too serious to trivialize. Eternity is at stake. I won't risk that."

"Come on, Cris." David poked his head through the open door, clearly miffed. "We need some serious Z's before we go over evidence, do edits, tape and do voice-overs."

Katherine smiled.

"Go, Cris Ocampo," Katherine whispered. "Know that many in both heaven and earth are grateful for your help and silence. Especially me. Go about living your life in peace."

"Come on, man," David complained. "It's six a.m. We have about a half hour drive to the hotel."

Cris caged Katherine in her chair. He leaned forward.

"You are an incredible and fascinating, woman, Katherine Gates. I'll keep your secrets, for now. But our discussion is in no way over. And, if you think this is the end, you are a fool. I will not let something so precious disappear from my life."

He looked at her, considering. Allowing free rein to a craving, his lips brushed hers in a soft glide. A different type of electricity sparked, invaded her nerve endings.

"Wanted to do that all night," Cris said and repeated it. "Nice."

Katherine sat, stunned. Watched him cross the room at a brisk pace, but pause at the open doorway. The megawatt smile was back in place, giving him an impish look.

"I'll be back," he told her. "Count on it."

Oh, my.

MIRROR, MIRROR:
A DETECTIVE NICK LARSON
STORY

DETECTIVE Nick Larson stood quietly in the middle of what, one week ago, had been a scene of carnage. Now, the bedroom resembled a crime scene still life, a macabre, frozen reminder of their investigation into the victim who had been brutalized at the hands of his wife.

Nick swallowed, remembering the smell of the scene. Damn. His reaction was always visceral. He was sensitive to the smells of death, even the memory of them. Always happened, and it sucked.

He started to sweat.

"You are not going to puke all over the scene, are you?" Sacco's voice grew stronger as he approached. As Nick's partner for close to six years, Sacco recognized the cues when Nick was about to hurl. "There's barely any smell left."

Nick turned. His smile was more a slit of deprecation.

"I'm fine."

"That's a relief," Sacco replied.

Side by side, both men stared at the room.

"What's wrong, Nick?"

Nick turned slightly. "Help me walk through this again, will you?"

"You can't be serious," Sacco said, his words basted with incredulity.

At Nick's continued silence, Sacco scratched his short, blonde buzz in visible frustration.

"Shit, Nick. This is an open and shut case. You can't seriously think she's not the killer?"

"Something doesn't feel right."

Sacco leaned forward, staring hard at Nick. "She's gotten to you, hasn't she? It's those eyes. You're letting a pair of eyes bring you down."

Nick stared at the bed across from him. That piece of furniture had been witness to a crime as brutal as Jack the Ripper's.

"Let's go through this, Vic, please." Nick knew Sacco would understand the request. He did this in cases that troubled him. His partner called it the scene talking to Nick.

Sacco stood silent for a minute.

"Okay," Sacco said and took out his notes.

"According to witnesses and employees, suspect's marriage was on the rocks. Rumor had it she was about to get a restraining order on the victim."

"Did we verify that?" Nick asked.

"Horowitz received a copy of the court filing yesterday."

"What's the story?"

"The suspect..."

"She has a name, you know," Nick said.

Vic shrugged. "According to the filing, Laura Howard stated her husband was, allegedly, getting abusive, in spite of the separation."

"So," Nick said and counted off on his fingers. "One: what was his business in her apartment that morning, and two, how did he get in?"

"NFC on the first. As to the second, Mrs. Howard's assistant confirmed Orlando Howard picked up the spare apartment key at her business. Claimed he had to get some legal papers."

Nick's cell phone rang. He glanced at the number and declined the call.

"Angie?" Sacco asked.

Nick nodded.

"What does she want now?"

"Same bull," Nick said, disgusted. His ex-wife was getting worse. And he was the stupid ass who kept helping her despite their divorce two years before.

"Okay. Supposedly, the victim comes to pick up legal papers..."

"Which we never found and Laura Howard denies ever having here," Sacco said.

Nick walked to the open closet doors.

"From the security camera video, Laura Howard, holding a kitchen knife, riffles through her clothes in the closet here." Nick stepped toward the bed. "When Orlando Howard enters the apartment, Laura Howard slides the knife between mattress and box spring." He imitated the action. "She leaves the handle halfway out, readily accessible, just in case she needs a weapon."

Sacco stood next to Nick. "She faces the door, waits for the victim to approach. Argument ensues."

"What are you doing here, you are my wife, yada yada," Nick said, imitating what he had seen replayed silently on the tape. "Things get physical. Anger becomes passion. Next thing you know, it's fornication at its rawest."

"Shit, Nick," Sacco grimaced. "I have an open mind, and occasionally enjoy a bout of rough, consensual sex. But this was animalistic to the max, bordering on brutal. If I hadn't seen her eager participation, riding him worse than a rodeo bull, I would have called it rape."

And the image of the woman on the video, humping the man with such gleeful ferocity, did not correlate with the one Nick had of shy, soft-spoken, classy Laura Howard. Somehow, deep in his gut, Nick thought the woman who was now their prime suspect wouldn't have behaved in such manner.

Yet the evidence said otherwise.

And that had his gut twisted worse than a knot.

As a homicide detective, experience had taught Nick not to take things at face value. Most crimes were not always as they seemed. Case in point: a year ago, they'd nabbed a serial killer who looked like a saint and had confessed his brutality in almost child-like candor and pride.

Yet, with this case, his instincts were clamoring worse than a five-alarm fire.

Another point of consideration was—what the hell did he know about women? Angela was the supreme example of his stupidity on the subject. She had been the essence of goodness and light, that is, before their marriage. After they'd tied the knot, the virago had slowly emerged, especially after the boozing and the drugs took hold, blaming her deterioration and all her misfortunes on him. On his job.

Nick's cell rang once more. He declined the call and rammed the thing down his pants pocket.

"Fast forward to a minute after climax," Nick continued. "Orlando Howard, instead of mellowing in his after-orgasm glow, is more pissed than ever. We don't know why."

"He throws suspect off the bed." Sacco pointed to a spot on the floor next to his feet. "She lands there."

"She's furious. Grabs the knife. And as Romeo begins to clean himself with the bedding, she slices and dices his privates, his stomach, his chest, and his face."

"What was the final knife count according to Totes?" Sacco asked. Totes was the affectionate nickname the department had given their medical examiner.

"Fifteen," Nick said, his face reflecting his disgust. He'd been the officer at autopsy. If it hadn't been for the mask sprayed with Febreze that camouflaged the smell of death, he would still be puking his guts out. "Five in the genitalia, four in the abdomen, four on the chest, and two on the face."

"Damn."

"Finally, Laura Howard conveniently drops the knife next to the victim's chopped manhood." Nick continued. "After that, we don't have any more info. She calmly walks to the security camera and shifts its angle to face the window. We presume she took a shower, changed clothes, and left for work like a cool cucumber. Five hours later, she issues the 911."

"Ballsy lady," Sacco said.

Nick scanned the room—closet, bathroom opening, bed, and dresser across from the bed.

"Why was the security camera moved after the killing?" Nick said. "What was she doing with a knife to begin with? And why was the soon-to-be ex so fucking pissed after roughrider sex? We're missing something here."

Sacco scanned the area. "Yeah. I see what you're getting at."

Nick pivoted. "I need to see that video again."

"Hey, Nick."

Nick stepped into the room where their lead Forensic Investigations Division evidence and fingerprint guru, Tish Ramos, stood cataloguing evidence. Items from their current case were organized in specific groupings on the worktable.

"Sacco said you wanted the video of the murder." She held up a sealed evidence bag and shook it. The lopsided flash drive inside settled to the bottom. "John Hancock, please."

"Word travels fast." Nick took his pen from inside his jacket and signed for it.

Ramos laughed. "Your gorgeous partner also said you are not sold on the evidence for this case."

"It should be a slam dunk, shouldn't it?" Nick said. "After all, the killer's face is full front and center on the video."

"Butchery et al caught in vivid, digital, reality show clarity," Ramos said and finished brushing the Bi-chromatic fingerprint powder on the security camera lens and housing collected from the bedroom of the Howard case. She stared at her results.

"But?" she asked, not paying attention to Larson but to the latent fingerprint the powder had revealed. She held two sizes of clear, lift tape, one in each hand, trying to decide which one would work best.

"Can't put my finger on it, yet."

Ramos raised a finger, her signal for Nick to wait. She chose a tape, discarded the other, and hovered it over the print with dead center precision. She pressed down. Nick admired the rock steadiness of her hands. Fingerprints were a bitch to process. Most of the time, they'd be lucky to get a usable partial. But Ramos had a gift. If anyone could get proof of identity through a fingerprint, it would be her.

Ramos lifted the tape in a slow, diagonal movement, pressed the print image on the backing of the card without getting her latex gloves snagged on it, and studied her handiwork. She grunted in satisfaction.

"A decent thumb print. Should get enough markers to confirm ID."

She turned to face Larson. "Is the woman still denying she murdered her ex?"

"Her lawyer is, adamantly so." Nick shook his head. "But you should have seen her at the arraignment. The woman looked as if a bomb had exploded next to her and she was still suffering from PTSD."

"When's the prelim?"

"In another seventy-two. Prosecutor is rushing. Captain is holding off for a confession. I say wishful thinking. But once the lawyer sees the entire video, plus all the other evidence, the prosecutor thinks they'll plead and avoid trial."

Ramos crooked a finger and scooted to the edge of her worktable.

"Well, sorry to add to your gut's woes." Ramos pointed to two crime scene photos and then to one article of clothing next to them. "By the way, trace is going over the material picked up on these, but that's not what I want to show you."

"What's the wait for DNA?"

"About a month...two," Ramos said. "DA isn't in a rush with this case."

"Because of the video evidence."

Ramos nodded. Nick joined her. She pointed to one of the photographs splayed on the table to her left.

"This," she pressed her forefinger to a dark lump visible near the edge of the victim's bed. "Is this." She followed words by tapping the blouse spread out on the table. "What do you see?"

Nick saw several neat rips and tears on the material. Otherwise, the blouse was clean, although rumpled. Nick surmised its state had to do with it being thrown on the bedroom floor like discarded refuse, as seen in the photograph.

"Apart from the obvious, I don't follow."

"What do you see around the tears, here and here?"

Nick reached for a pair of gloves, snapped them on, and picked up the blouse, studied the cuts. "Nothing."

Ramos beamed at him, as though he was her best intern.

"Exactly. These cuts," she pointed, "were created with a knife."

"Not scissors?"

Ramos looked at him as if he'd just insulted her, which, to a point, he had.

"Edges neat, not ribbed. Width is a perfect match to the width of your murder weapon. But," and here Ramos faced him, her eyes intent. "There is no blood around the tears. There is no blood anywhere except for some castoff on the back of the blouse, which was the only side exposed during the murder. This defacing was done before the murder. I bet my ass on it."

"And it's such a nice one, according to Sacco."

Ramos laughed, punched his arm, pivoted, and picked another crime scene photograph, this time taken in the living room. She handed it to Nick, pointing to the sofa.

"Look." Anticipating his next question, Ramos handed over her magnifying glass.

He picked up on her cue. Small pieces of batting from inside the leather sofa backrest littered the seat cushion directly below. One or two were visible from what looked like a tear on the headrest.

"I bet when I go back to the crime scene to measure those tears, they'll match the blouse's exact slicing pattern, position of cuts, and width of blade."

"That answers one of my questions."

"Why she had a knife in the bedroom?"

"Yeah," Nick said and picked up the evidence bag with the flash drive. "But the better question is: why the hell would this woman want to destroy her own clothes?"

Nick was about to hook the flash drive to his computer when the desk phone rang.

"Larson."

"You are a bastard, Nicky. Why haven't you answered my calls?"

Shit. Angela.

Nick walked around his desk and, with his foot, closed the door to the office.

"Angie, I'm in the middle of a homicide. I'm busy."

"You're always too goddamn busy for me." Angela's voice changed tenor, a mix of whine and plea. "He's left me, Nick. Dumped me like used toilet paper for a twenty-three-year-old ass."

"Angie..."

"I can't take this anymore. Why does everyone leave me?"

Nick didn't point out she usually did the dumping and, in the past two years, Angela had changed lovers more times than underwear. Unfortunately, the last asshole she'd hooked up with was an occasional user, whose wants superseded her own. And Angela had to be the center of attention, the focus and the need.

"I want to see you."

He almost asked why but said, "I've got a case to solve and it can't wait. Are you at work?"

Her silence told him no. She'd probably lose this job, again, the third one he'd gotten her this year.

"Well, it's not as if I could go in looking like shit."

Sacco banged on the office window, motioned to the briefing room.

"Come to me, Nicky," she said, trying to be seductive, but ruining it with the constant sniffles and slurred voice.

"Go sleep off whatever you're on. Call your sponsor. Get help. I've gotta go."

"Save me?"

Nick was bone tired, soul tired of this repetitive singsong. It had been going on for two years. At first, right after the divorce, he'd fallen for her plea every single time, sometimes going back to her, believing maybe they could work through their issues. But after six months of additional hell, with her drinking more out of control, her stealing to get high more evident, and her constant threats getting progressively worse, he'd had enough.

"You don't want to be saved, Angie." His voice held the usual mix of frustrated anger and sadness directed at this woman who only wanted to self-destruct at his expense. "You want to rip and drag me to your level. I'm tired of this shit. Go bleed someone else."

"You owe me, you bastard."

"I don't owe you jack shit."

"If it weren't for you, I wouldn't need..."

"This is bullshit."

Nick slammed the receiver on its cradle, grabbed the Howard murder three-ring binder, and stormed out of the office. In the briefing room, he slammed the binder on the table and sat.

Sacco almost whistled, but kept it to himself.

"Angela's latest dumped her," Nick volunteered before Sacco could question him.

"No wonder your phone's been ringing at all hours."

"Yeah. I've become the flavor of the moment."

Ramos arrived, her arm cradling her evidence binder. "Shame you can't commit her." She'd heard Nick's last words. "She needs serious psychiatric help."

Captain Kravitz strode in. "Let's hustle, people. Have a meet with the DA in fifty, and traffic's a bitch going crosstown."

"You want to give him the good news?" Ramos asked, looking at Nick.

Kravitz stared Ramos down.

"Oh, hell no." His eyes pierced every single person in the room. When he saw Larson's face, Kravitz threw up his arms and dropped on the chair. "Please tell me you are, in no fucking way, questioning culpability?"

"Captain..." Nick started.

Ramos interrupted. "In all fairness to Larson here, Captain, we just discovered some discrepancies with the evidence."

"You've got to be shitting me." Kravitz's jaw worked. If he'd been smoking his favorite cigars, he would have chewed the end off. "What discrepancy can there be after the video evidence?"

"A few things are bugging me, have been bugging me for a while," Nick said. "Why, if this Howard woman did not know her husband would appear that day, did she carry a knife into the bedroom? Why did the soon-to-be ex go apeshit after sex? Why did she change the security camera angle after the killing? Why is the timeline of some witness statements off? And then there is what Ramos found."

Ramos cut in. "Digging through the evidence this morning, I found a blouse whose material was ripped, possibly by the murder weapon. The area around the cut, however, was clean of blood, even when that piece of evidence was discovered at the foot of the bed." Ramos took the photograph of the living room couch and showed it to Kravitz. "You can see the couch has evidence of cuts. I made a paper pattern of the blouse with the tears and the dimensions of the cuts, and will go back to the crime scene after our briefing to compare notes."

"I'll be reviewing all the apartment's security video now, too." Nick pointed his chin at Sacco. "Vic can review the surveillance tapes we got hold of today around the apartment area, and in the woman's business. Maybe we can figure what was going on."

"Captain," Ramos asked. "Is there any way we can get a priority on the DNA for this case? There is no way in hell that she did not cut herself while butchering her ex. Her hand must have been slipping and sliding on all that blood."

Nick turned to Sacco. "Did we take any pics of her hands when we booked her?"

Sacco shook his head.

"Get that woman into interrogation, now," Kravitz said. He turned to Ramos. "If she wielded the knife, there should still be evidence of cuts on her hands. Get it."

Kravitz glanced at all. "Anything else?"

Everyone shook their heads, stood, and went to work.

"Look at this."

Sacco lifted his head. He'd been looking through surveillance tapes for an hour. He'd captured their killer in several of them and had jotted down the digital markers so the lab could convert the images there to printed photographs.

Nick turned the monitor toward his partner. "Once Ramos told me about the blouse, I went back to the video of the living room-kitchen area." With a pinkie, he pointed to the screen.

"Watch." Nick clicked the play button.

The upper corner of the front door opened and Laura Howard walked inside. But instead of doing things like most normal people would do entering their homes, this Laura Howard roamed the area, caressing the furniture with loving fingers. She paused by the sofa, picked up the blouse there, and pressed her palm against it. She smiled and strode to the kitchen. She rummaged inside the refrigerator, drank from the orange juice carton, and dumped the rest of the juice in the sink. She lifted several knives from the holder on the counter, chose a wide blade one, and walked to the sofa. There she stretched the blouse flat, and proceeded to slash it.

Nick stopped the tape.

"That's one fucked-up crazy woman," Sacco said.

Nick minimized the window from that portion of the security camera video and maximized another screen. It showed the bedroom. According to the counter stamped at the bottom right, only a few minutes between the scene in the living room and this one had elapsed.

"There she is again, at the closet, knife in hand. I think she is riffling through the clothes to do the same thing she did to the blouse. This time, however, she's interrupted."

Both men watched silently. There was the moment when Laura Howard's body language showed she'd been alerted to a noise. She walked to the bed, placed the knife under the mattress and waited.

Nick fast-forwarded to the first altercation.

"Here," Nick pointed to where the ex-husband's hands were. "He grabs her by the wrists. Violently. She should have bruises from that, too. But I don't remember seeing any on her wrists and forearms."

"According to Horowitz, Laura Howard is being processed right now. He'll call us when it's done."

Nick fast-forwarded to the end of the sexual act. He didn't want to witness that again. He already had a vivid image of it imprinted on his brain.

"This is what I don't get." He paused the video before the ex throws his wife on the floor. Replays it in slow motion. "The man is really pissed. Shouts something at her."

Sacco moved closer to the screen. "Super pissed, if body language is anything."

Nick stopped the video and considered. "Isn't Mandy Penzik a hearing impaired advocate?"

Sacco nodded. Mandy had a deaf son. She had been instrumental at court and at interrogations whenever they had needed help with the hearing impaired.

Nick poked his head outside the office door. "Swan," he yelled. "Find Penzik for me, would you? Need her expertise on something."

Nick played the rest of the video. The killing was savage, but the only flash of rage from the woman was not while she was massacring the man. It was at the moment of rejection, or disgust, by the ex-husband. Everything that followed was done in clinical detachment.

They watched her drop the knife, go to the surveillance camera and shift it.

"Why the hell does she do that?" Nick said, more baffled now than before.

"I don't get it, either, but..." Sacco turned his computer screen to face Larson. "It may explain something." He pointed to two paused video windows side by side.

"They're a bit grainy," Sacco said, pointing to the two images of the same woman. "But this Laura Howard on the right is not wearing the same outfit as the Laura Howard on the left. As a matter of fact," he flipped through the murder binder, took out the mug shot of their murder suspect.

"Laura Howard is not wearing either of the outfits when brought in for questioning a couple of hours later."

"What the..."

"Hey, Nick, Sacco. What do you need?"

Mandy Penzik looked more like an anchorwoman from a glitzy entertainment TV show rather than a seasoned police sergeant with ten years experience on the force.

"Hey, gorgeous," Sacco said. "How's your son?"

"Eddie's fine. Graduates in a couple of weeks, then off to college in a few more. Damn, but I'm going to miss him."

Nick's cell phone pinged. He looked at the screen and cursed. Angela was now calling him using Facetime. He hated these damn smart phones where no one had time to piss in privacy. He dropped the phone on the desk, ignoring the incessant vibrating echoes.

"Do you read lips?"

"Sure. Why?"

"See if you can figure out what this man's saying."

Nick rewound the tape to the moment after climax. Played it. Mandy's face was a study in concentration.

"Can you play it again, but this time zoom in, if you can."

"It may fuzz the image a bit."

"Try anyway."

Nick zoomed and replayed. Mandy watched.

"Who the fuck are you?" she said. "You talk, talk. Get, something, something, something, and then me." She looked at Nick. "Does that help?"

"Are you sure?"

"About the who the bleep are you? Yeah. Can't say about the rest. Her body gets in the way more than once before I can see his lips again."

Mandy pointed to the computer screen. "Is this the Howard case?"

"Turning out to be more like a messed up Jekyll and Hyde case, if you ask me," Sacco said.

"Thought it was a slam dunk," she said, looking at both men.

"So did we," Nick answered. "Unless she's Machiavellian and playing us for fools. It wouldn't be the first time."

"There are some seriously fucked-up people out there," Mandy agreed.

Nick's phone vibrated again.

Case in point. His ex-wife.

"Angela's not going to stop until you answer," Sacco told him.

"I don't give a shit."

Horowitz poked his head into the office. "Carpenter's done, Lieutenant. He's waiting for you outside interrogation one."

Nick and Sacco thanked Mandy and walked to where Carpenter, crime scene techie, waited for them, his digital camera at the ready.

"Here's what I got."

Nick and Sacco gathered around the viewfinder. Carpenter began flipping photographs. No bruising anywhere. A few nicks and cuts on her hands, though.

"Wait. Go back."

Carpenter skimmed backward until Nick stopped him.

"What is that?" he pointed to the right thumb of the woman's hand.

"She has some sort of scar there. Keeps worrying it with the nails of her middle and forefinger." Carpenter looked at them. "If she doesn't stop doing that soon, she'll bleed all over your interrogation room."

"Print for me what you took." Nick looked at Sacco. "Tell Ramos I need her to compare the fingerprint she lifted from the security camera with Laura Howard's booking prints. We need answers."

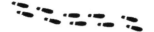

Laura Howard didn't know if she was going to puke, faint, or die of a heart attack in this miserable little hole-in-the-wall of an interrogation room. She'd been here before. Remembered the two detectives plowing at her mercilessly, trying to trip her, make her confess to a crime she knew she had not committed. She'd been furious they hadn't believed her at first. The fury and denials had turned into silence and incredulity as they described her behavior at the apartment, into humiliation when shown the sexually explicit photos of her banging her husband, and into shocked horror at the images of what she'd purportedly done to the man she had loved until recently.

If she had not seen her face reflected back at her, she would have sworn someone was playing a nasty joke on her.

After that, she'd been in a sort of daze for her booking and her arraignment. Now she'd been dragged in here once again, her arms and hands placed under the glaring lens of another camera, to be studied and scrutinized under the microscope of supposed culpability.

Her lawyer said these people had irrefutable proof of her guilt and were pushing for her to plead to a lesser charge. So was he. She almost laughed aloud. Manslaughter instead of murder one. Legally, the dividing line was a big one, especially in her sentencing. Morally, murder was murder. Orlando was dead. What did it matter if legalese said she had done it in premeditation or in a jealous rage?

Her husband would still be dead.

Butchered.

Skinned.

Oh, God.

Her stomach heaved. She grabbed the nearest wastebasket and dry retched until her stomach settled. She spit out what saliva she had on top of the miserable drop of bile inside the trash. She scanned the room, saw no tissues around, and used her jail-issued pantsuit sleeve to clean her lips. She was a jailbird now. A felon. It didn't matter if she smelled like shit until she was allowed to wash or change her clothes.

She wished she were dead.

The door opened and one of the two detectives who'd interrogated her earlier stood framed there. He was the handsome one, the one with the sad eyes, soft voice. He smelled nice. He'd treated her with respect, unlike the other one, who looked more like he'd been the high school bully from the football team.

What was this man's name? Larson, she remembered. Detective Larson.

The nice one.

She shook her head. Who the hell was she kidding? He probably was as hard an ass as detectives came, a bastard in disguise, waiting to break her until she wouldn't be able to put the pieces of her soul back together.

He walked into the room. Quietly, he placed a three-ring binder on the table. He removed a pen from his shirt pocket, together with a small flip notebook, and placed that next to the binder. He flipped open an old laptop computer, sat, and leaned back, studying her.

She waited.

His move.

He stared at her for what seemed forever. Then stared at her arms for another lifetime, then at her hands.

She jumped when he spoke.

"You cut your hands. How?"

Laura stared at her hands, saw the usual cuts and nicks from her trade. Well, what used to be her trade. Her business, a high-end bakery, *Les Gateaux Riches*, specializing in wedding cakes and other baked goods for an exclusive clientele, would probably end up in the hands of her associate now.

"I bake and design cakes for a living." She turned her hands over and back again. "I always have nicks and cuts."

"You don't remember where you got those?" Nick's voice was deceptively calm.

Laura shook her head and waited. She began to pick at the keloid on her right thumb. She'd gotten the scar tissue when she'd almost sliced her thumb through and through when eight years old. Whenever she was stressed or nervous, she would pick at it until the area became raw.

"Can I show you something?"

Laura stared.

Nick turned the computer screen on. He played the security video of her apartment's living room first. Then sat back to observe her responses.

Nick had seen faked reactions before. Had seen drama and acting. The confusion on this woman's face, transforming into a shock so intense a moment later, could not be faked. And the expression in her eyes, incredulous and agonized at the same time, disturbed him.

The section of video stopped. Nick waited.

"That was...it couldn't have been." Laura shook her head, as if trying to clear her thoughts. "I don't remember..."

"You don't remember cutting up your blouse?"

She looked at Nick, her eyes huge.

"No," she whispered. "That wasn't me. Couldn't have been me." With a stronger voice, she almost shouted. "That wasn't me. You Photoshopped that. You're tricking me."

Nick clicked on the other open window screen and hit play.

Laura's eyes were drawn back to the computer.

She saw the woman that was her, yet not her, walk to the closet, riffle through her clothes. Saw this impostor hide under the mattress the knife she'd taken from *her* kitchen, saw the confrontation with *her* husband. Then she saw the rest and she thought she would die. She turned to the wastebasket she'd placed on the floor and threw up more bile.

Nick paused the video and looked up at the camera in the room. "Bring some water and tissues," he said. Nick knew Sacco would follow his request.

"This wasn't Photoshopped, Laura," Nick said.

"But that's not me," she said, her voice soft, her tone incredulous. "It can't be me. I, I am not that monster."

Nick pointed to the paused screen. Laura's face was staring at the camera, her right hand poised to move it. "Are you telling me this isn't you?"

Laura stared at her face, which was not *her* face. Was she mad? Was she in a living nightmare? She'd heard about those. Or maybe stress had finally taken its toll and turned her insane without her even knowing it? Was she one of these people who sleepwalked and did unspeakable things while in that state? Or was she a Ted Bundy in the making?

Nick's phone started ringing. She saw him look at the touch screen. His lips became a slit of disapproval before ignoring the call and concentrating on her.

"Come on, Laura. Why did you do it? Was he getting violent? Threatening?"

Laura remained silent. Tears pooled and dropped silently onto her cheeks, her lips, her chest. She didn't move.

"We have a copy of the restraining order," Nick continued. "What did he do to you for you to want to retaliate so brutally?"

Laura shivered and rubbed her arms in reaction. She remembered the last time Orlando had caught her unaware, unprepared. He'd forced himself on her, thinking the violence of his action would somehow make her more pliable, more manageable.

Make her return to him, depend on him.

What it had done was make her spitting mad.

It had humiliated her beyond repair.

But would she have retaliated by killing him? Had she done that?

The other detective stepped inside with a box of tissues and a bottle of water. Left everything in front of her and, without uttering a word, exited the room. Nick opened the bottle for her and pushed the tissue box near her. She grabbed a tissue, cleaned her face and blew her nose.

"You know," Nick said, getting comfortable in his chair. "I can understand rough play. It can lead to very good sex."

Nick watched Laura's face blanch, then turn beet red. Interesting.

"But what I don't get is—what did you say to Orlando that got him so pissed he threw you to the floor?"

Laura shook her head. Began crying in earnest.

The detective's phone rang.

He almost turned it off but paused when he read what was flashing on the screen.

"Excuse me for a moment."

He stepped outside, where Sacco waited. He put the call on speaker.

"Talk to me."

"It isn't her, Nick."

Sacco was the first to react. "What the hell do you mean it's not her."

"It's not her. Wait for me. I'm on my way."

They gathered in the conference room—Kravitz, Nick, Ramos, and Sacco.

"Okay, Ramos," Kravitz said. "Spill."

Ramos placed the fingerprint card with Laura Howard's prints in front of the men. "We took these when we booked her for murder. Look at both thumb prints."

Nick studied the prints. He saw the black ridge created by the scar on the right thumb. The left one was normal.

Next, Ramos showed them the card with the fingerprint she'd lifted that morning.

"This is the latent print I got from the security camera, the one in her bedroom."

"Okay," Sacco said, after a cursory inspection of the material in front of him. "It's a partial, but it doesn't seem to have a ridge through it. So it's her left thumb print."

"Wrong."

Ramos lifted her computer lid and opened her comparison software. She dragged the scanned fingerprint from the camera and compared it, first to Laura's right thumb, then her left. No match. She glanced at the men, expecting the light of comprehension to shine from their faces.

"Gentlemen, come on. There is only one possibility." She ticked off the answers on her fingers. "What looks alike, has the same DNA, not that that's going to do us any good now, but doesn't share the same fingerprints?"

Nick gasped. "Twins? The woman on the video is Laura Howard's twin?"

"It's either that," Ramos said with satisfaction, "or this person went through extensive facial reconstruction for the bitch of it."

"You've got to be shitting me," Kravitz erupted.

"It's the only thing that makes sense, Captain," Nick said.

"According to the background done, she doesn't have any siblings," Sacco said.

"We're going to have to dig deeper." Nick looked at all of them. "Adoptions, juvie records, fosters. There's got to be something."

"I'll run the print through AFIS," Ramos said. "We might get lucky."

"In the meantime," Kravitz said. "Howard stays in holding. I'll talk to the DA, see what he wants done."

"And we have to process the scene all over again," Nick told Ramos. "See if you can get more prints on the objects this other woman touched in that apartment. I'll give you a list after I catalogue everything from the video. We need to separate the real Laura Howard from the fake one."

Ramos stopped Nick from leaving. She turned the computer screen to face him. It showed the woman, who was not Laura Howard, frozen in time by technology as she reached out to turn the security camera's angle. Ramos pointed to the hand, highlighted the area she wanted, and zoomed. The thumb of the right hand came into focus.

No scar.

"You and your gut," Ramos said, admiration toning her voice. "Remind me never to bet against it."

It took a week, literally, of pounding the pavement, but they found the twin in a seedy Bowery hotel that served hookers, druggies, and overall low lives. Basically, the way she'd lived all her life, according to the background they'd dug on her. Now, armed with partials and new evidence, the woman, a Sandra Ward, waited in the same interrogation room they had taken Laura Howard a week ago.

Nick sat facing her, disturbed by the uncanny replication of one human being to another. Hair color, eye color, brow, nose, and lip shape, and the placement of a small mole on the upper right corner of the upper lip, were identical. Height, weight: similar. Even hairstyles had been imitated.

Only thing separating these twins were dental records, fingerprints, and...

The eyes.

Sandra Ward's eyes, as they looked at Nick, spoke of lifelong hustling, of cynicism, of street experience. Uncaring eyes. Selfish eyes, focused inward. Jealous eyes, focused outward. Opportunistic eyes. Calculating eyes.

Angela's eyes.

Maybe that was why he'd reacted so negatively to the possibility of Laura Howard committing such heinous murder. Why he had questioned. Laura's eyes had not reflected the sleaziness of life reflected back at him from the woman facing him.

Nick waited and observed. Uncanny how he had no doubt this Sandra Ward, who faced him now as if nothing were happening, was capable of murder. Hell, had murdered Orlando Howard without compunction.

The question was, why?

Nick took out his phone and shut it off. He didn't want any interruptions, at least not from Angela. Her harassing calls had multiplied, she'd lost her job, and now she was using a new manipulative tactic—threatening to kill herself if he didn't pay attention to her needs. Just this week, she had fooled him with a fake suicide, twice. She'd abused 911 resources to get his attention. Had even come to his workplace and created a scene to end all scenes.

He'd had it. Wouldn't put up with the bullshit, not any more.

Nick opened the Howard file. "Were your rights read?"

Sandra Ward lifted a brow, her eyes scornful. She leaned back in her chair and crossed her legs in a provocative pose.

Sacco had prepared a grouping of photographs for this interrogation. Nick took them out of the binder and scanned them quickly.

"Can I ask you something?"

Nick placed the top photograph in front of her.

"You entered Ms. Howard's apartment at ten-oh-five in the morning."

Another photo appeared next to the first one.

"You roamed the living area, caressed the furniture."

She smirked at his use of the word caress.

"Drank some juice. Chose a knife at random."

Nick laid the next three photos below the others facing her.

"You then hacked the blouse as if it were a living thing, went into the bedroom, hid the knife, and confronted Mr. Howard."

Another three photographs were placed below the previous ones.

"Things got rough, sex was...energetic."

"Very," she said.

"But then something goes wrong." Nick tapped one photograph in particular. "Mr. Howard was somehow on to you. Asked who you were."

Sandra Ward chuckled. "Actually, he said, and I quote, Who the fuck are you?"

Nick set the photograph with her sprawled on the floor after Mr. Howard threw her there. She leaned forward a bit, glided her fingers over her image.

"What set you off?" Nick asked, and followed words with three more shots of her brutalizing Mr. Howard.

"I reminded him I was his wife, but he didn't buy it. Didn't care who the hell I was. I tried to get him to fuck me again but, instead, he said not to waste his time. His wife was a better ride. He was going to call the police if I didn't get the fuck out, but, especially, he said he had no use for a whore like me."

The look she turned on Nick was hard, a give no quarter kind of look.

"No one uses and discards me. No one."

The lady was some number. Nick placed the last photograph on the table. It was of her reaching for the surveillance camera in order to move it.

"Now this photo baffles me Sandra. Why on earth did you do this?"

The woman shrugged. "The show was over. *She* had seen *me,* what I had done. What I could do. And I had just ruined her perfect little life forever." She stared at Nick. "A little tit-for-tat. Never thought you'd figure things out."

And thank God they had.

THE END

EVERYONE'S A CRITIC

AN idea took shape... was developed... shaped...
Conflicts arose: Sufferings, joys, struggles, and love...
Strength rose from adversity, life became—breathed.
Splendor and simplicity was revealed...
Triumph over hardship shown.
Then...
It's too long, keep it simple...
It's too short.
Too much suffering... Not enough—why not?
Too much sex... not enough.
Too stupid to live...
Too macho for me...
Cut the adverbs and write in one view...
Conflict too overdone, overused...
Enough with the fantasy, enough with the wolves.
Enough with the vampires that don't act as they should.
Setting too extravagant... too clichéd.
I could solve the problem in a much faster way...
And so it goes...
Therefore...
There once was a woman who met a man...
They lived in a beautiful place, wherever you want...
With no troubles, no flaws, no conflict, no lies...
They met, had mind-blowing sex...
And lived happily ever after.
There.

The End.

ABOUT THE AUTHOR

Maria Elena Alonso-Sierra is a romantic suspense author with a unique point of view. Her adventure novels take place in locales across Europe and the United States, reflecting her international upbringing and extensive time as a global traveler. In her duology, *The Coin* and *The Book of Hours*, her characters, Gabriela and Richard, walk the same paths as their creator, though her life was never in so much danger.

In her short story collection, *The Fish Tank: And Other Short Stories*, she lets her imagination flow in every genre (from paranormal to mystery) and writes fictional representation of real events suffered by the Cuban Diaspora, of which she weaves many of her own experiences into the stories.

Ms. Alonso-Sierra's writing career began circa age thirteen with a very juvenile science fiction short story, but the writing bug hit, and she has been writing, in one capacity or another, ever since. She has worked as a professional dancer, singer, journalist, and literature teacher (and not necessarily in that order—she likes variety) and holds a Masters in English literature. She loves to hear from readers and, when not writing, roams around to discover new places to set her novels.

Her detective novel, Hanging Softly in the Night, has received several awards and been described as, "a written version of CSI:New York with an added dose of crazy."

Ms. Alonso-Sierra is currently working on her next novel and lives in Florida with her husband and her dog, Amber.

Connect with the author at the following:

Website: https://mariaelenawrites.com

Blog: https://mariaelenawrites.com/blog

Facebook:
https://facebook.com/MariaElenaAlonsoSierraWrites

Twitter: https://twitter.com/MariaElenaWrite

Goodreads:
https://www.goodreads.com/author/show/7093896.Maria_
Elena_Alonso_Sierra

If you enjoyed *The Fish Tank: And Other Short Stories,* here is a peek at other works by the same author.

THE COIN - BOOK 1
International Romantic Suspense, set in the beautiful French Riviera.

Can finding a coin get you killed?

THE COIN

For a preview, turn the page...

For a preview, turn the page...

PROLOGUE

France, May 1993

HE was safe.

The man surveyed the clearing, inspecting the rearranged landscape for the last time. The mounds of rock and dirt surrounding him dropped unevenly, pock-marking the ground in no visible pattern. Nature had spread her hand, healing the upheaval she'd caused a year ago by covering the ground with short-cropped grass, dehydrated moss, bramble, lavender, thyme and the local version of oregano bushes. There was no evidence anywhere of his search, past or present, nor did the metal detector sound any signal of Nature regurgitating the remaining strongbox it had so callously devoured.

The man's hands curled around the plastic bar of the metal detector, tightening into a fist so fierce his forearms vibrated. Years of planning, of careful manipulation, of evidence gathering, of assuring no one could trace the puppeteer pulling the strings of mayhem, had been nullified without trace by the whim of a capricious mountain. Even when luck had remained stubbornly by his side, helping him recuperate many of his records and videotapes, he'd only gathered a pittance of the arsenal he'd had. If Nature had been a real woman standing before him, he thought, he would have relished killing her.

He skimmed the area once again, his eyes methodically covering more ground, his features darkened by the approaching twilight. His job here was almost over. After this final sweep, he could finally disappear and begin to plot again.

"Oh, danke Gott."

The strange voice caught him by surprise. He whirled around to face the intruder, his body rigid. A wiry young man, looking tired and terribly frustrated, now stood a few paces into the clearing. The man watched as the hiker shrugged off his bulky backpack, grabbed his knees for support, and gulped down several cool breaths of mountain air, grateful for the respite and his luck.

"Please forgive me," the hiker said, his French atrocious. "I've been roaming this godforsaken mountain for hours and can't seem to get back on the trail." His gaze turned hopeful. "Can you help me?"

The man nodded, but his eyes narrowed, intent on this intruder, this new threat to his carefully plotted safety net. He began to close in slowly.

The hiker visibly relaxed. "Thank God. I thought I'd be forced to camp out tonight."

The mouth and eyes that smiled back at the hiker chilled the surrounding air. The man loved fools such as this hiker, blind idiots who never suspected a normal façade could harbor the blackest of souls. Such naïveté always delighted him, made his hands itch with the anticipation of the kill. But for now, he gestured to his left, toward a dirt path barely visible through the trees.

As expected, the hiker turned, eager for directions. The man's smile widened. He lifted the metal detector.

The calculated blow to the head was swift, but not lethal. The hiker stumbled, caught off guard. The man waited patiently for his victim to recognize the danger, for the eyes to widen with dawning horror, and for the futile attempt to flee. Staggering, disoriented, the hiker backed away from what he now realized was a man gone mad. Smiling, the man lifted and struck again, this time on the upper arm. A whimper rose to a wail that bounced over the mountain. The man closed in once more, considering several options. With calculating precision, he aimed at the hiker's left thigh, reveled as he felt the femur collapse with a soft, moist crack. The hiker screamed, tumbling into a wriggling heap on the ground. The man swung again and struck his victim's abdomen. He watched the hiker painfully inch backward. Such foolishness, the man thought. Escape was impossible. No amount of begging, sobbing, or sniveling would stop him—had ever stopped him. The laughter he'd held back bubbled and spewed forth, noxious, tainting the surrounding air. He lifted the metal detector and struck again, and again, and again, calculating the most effective areas to hit, watching his victim with a chilling, benign emptiness. The macabre choreography increased the man's joy as each blow landed. By the time the man was satisfied, the hiker's agony had shifted from screams, to supplications, and finally to barely audible moans, twitches, and sobs.

The man paused, evaluating his handiwork. Bruises and hematomas discolored the exposed skin on the hiker's body. Perfection, he thought. Utter perfection. Later, under cover of darkness, he would take his burden and toss him down the ravine underneath the village of Gourdon. He chuckled. The stupid *gendarmes* would label the death a hiking accident. His only concern was that dead men didn't talk, or point accusing fingers at anyone.

His cold eyes swept over the hiker. Yes, he would do. He dropped the metal detector and stretched, ignoring the pathetic twitching and sobbing of the young man at his feet. He inhaled deeply, reveling in the pungent perfume of the pine trees mixed with that of human fear and excrement. Yes, everything was in order, he thought, pleased, as he knelt beside his victim. With strong arms, he captured the hiker's head in a chokehold. He caressed the hiker's face, grabbed his chin, and gave the head a vicious twist. The neck snapped like a soda cracker.

Oblivious now to the lifeless heap at his feet, the man examined the clearing in the rapidly fading light. He reached into his pocket and retrieved a ten franc 1945 French coin, no longer in circulation. His fingers lovingly caressed the etched image of Napoleon, and thought that his only regret was not finding the coins, his unique password. He'd keep this last one as his lucky charm, and start over again.

But that was for the future. For now, he was safe.

THE BOOK OF HOURS – BOOK 2
Romantic suspense, set in California and London.

Can psychopaths hit twice? A manuscript, a secret, and a few hours to live.

Make sure to pick up the sequel to *The Coin:*
The Book of Hours

For a preview, turn the page...

PROLOGUE

Monterey Bay, California 1997

THE past, figuratively, had been stooping over Gabriela Martinez's shoulder all morning long. Now it rode copilot on the drive home, laughing like a psychotic macaw at her feeble attempts to staunch the memories.

Hell. It was not as if this battle was new. For four years, Gabriela had been sparring with her past and its mockery, its unexpected hounding, its inconvenient ambushes, and its vicious pouncing with a relentless force of will. It was harassment, plain and simple, implacable, the transformative memories slithering unbidden into her consciousness: a soft caress that made her tremble, gray eyes that bored into her soul, arms that held softly or protected, and, oh God, lips that made her feel things she had never felt in all her married life.

That's because it wasn't your husband who made you feel them, her past snickered.

Well, hell. Score.

Past: one. Gabriela: zero.

She rammed the clutch. She really needed to snap out of this self-pity buffet she was dishing out today. With a practiced move, Gabriela downshifted to second and the BMW sedan slowed on cue. She veered southbound onto the last leg of her journey home, grateful she was only a few miles away. Focus, she ordered. Time to snap out of my-life-is-just-a-smorgasbord-of-misery crap. Today, she didn't have time for self-pity or memory lane flashbacks. Now that her meeting about the upcoming auction with her manager, Jean-Louis, was over, she had a nightmare of scheduling to organize. There was no time for the past and her thoughts. The better and more efficient undertaking was to keep the gear in second, give her brakes some respite, and focus on this downward gradient of road, which had more twists than a pretzel.

Brave words, her past intruded, then proceeded to remind her exactly who was in charge. Because when she looked about at the trees bordering the road, at the granite peeking out from behind curtains of pines, bushes, and dark earth, she was reminded of another similar road, another similar drive four years ago.

With Richard.

Damn.

Another score.

Past: two. Gabriela: zilch.

Renewed pain pierced her at the fleeting thought of Richard, launching once more a gamut of emotions—pleasure, longing, and heartbreak—some worse than others, and all linked to her memories of him. The worst were the constant yearnings entangled with a sense of abandonment, which wasn't fair, either. Hadn't Richard asked her to eliminate all doubts before reaching out to him, free and clear, with no regrets? She'd been working on exactly that for the past four years, and God only knew she had tried to keep her marriage afloat. But something in her relationship with her husband had splintered even before Richard had appeared in her life back in 1993. Had been irrevocably fractured in France, where her life had been threatened and almost snuffed out. And now in California shattered beyond redemption. There would be no turning back. And through it all, this piercing silence from Richard had been crushing. Year after year, she increasingly suspected his proclamation of undying love and the, *I love you with a terrible need,* had been crap written on paper. She feared Richard had moved on with his life, had married, and had a family of his own. *Forgotten her,* came the awful whisper. Unlike her. And during those moments, supposedly brave Gabriela turned into a veritable wimp.

He could be dead because of his job.

The car swerved.

Damn.

Score another hit for her past.

Three versus zero.

Gabriela straightened the Beemer and made a concerted effort to pay attention to her driving. That last thought had shaken her, badly. She tapped the brakes before the next curve. The response was slower than usual. Hell. What now? Her mechanic had finished servicing the car not two days ago and had boasted it drove like a dream machine. If he had overlooked some stupid thing, it would place the final cherry on top of her life's bitter sundae.

She took her foot off the accelerator and let the gearshift slow the car's momentum.

For a minute or two, she hummed along with the Vivaldi concerto on the radio's classical channel, a lame attempt to distract herself for a bit. But her thoughts refused to follow this new path, wandering back, once more, into familiar territory. Why on earth did she keep fighting herself, her memories? Why on earth didn't she *do* something, finally? She had her answer for Richard, but she now needed his. Jean-Louis had been after her for over a week on that subject. But she wasn't sure reaching out was a good idea. Not yet. Frankly, she was afraid to hope, and downright afraid, period. And ever since that desolate day at the *Marbriére*, she wouldn't be able to deal with a final rejection or abandonment from Richard as well. Besides, she wasn't free to make any kind of decision at the moment, either. Which brought her full circle. Why the hell did she continue this farce? Why on earth did she keep going back, day after day, to visit Roberto?

Gabriela's breath hitched as she tried to suppress her tears. Did she really believe things would end well and she could finally be free?

Guilt brings no freedom, a ghostly whisper teased her brain.

Round four, hands down, to the past, the nasty bastard.

Double damn.

Gabriela sighed. The ache in her soul felt like a sprain in need of Bengay. Guilt—the other taskmaster from hell. It hovered like a miniature avenging angel, lacerating her conscience every single day. Slash. You fell in love with another man. Slash. You gave birth to that man's child. Slash. You kept the child's identity a secret. But the biggest whiplash was asking Roberto for a divorce the same day he wound up in a coma.

Gabriela's thoughts screeched to a halt. *Whoa. Just one damn minute,* she told herself. *Let's be honest here.* She did not feel guilt at asking for the divorce, just guilt at her timing. Gabriela actually owed Roberto a grateful 'thanks' for plopping the overflow drop into the bucket of her restraint. Nothing attached her to him anymore, except Robertico and Gustavito, their two teenage sons, and Luisito, her energetic three-year-old. Gabriela hadn't even been upset by the fact Roberto had taken a mistress—had been sleeping with the woman for over four months, to be exact. On that day of confrontation, Gabriela had finally realized her marriage was indeed dead, with nothing worthwhile to rescue except the children.

She had felt no jealousy at Roberto's admission, just a boatload of sadness at the waste of it all. And, if she were equally, brutally honest with herself, she had remained with Roberto this long simply because life had taken over, with routine and comfort replacing love and passion.

And you wanted to make sure there was nothing left in the marriage, as Richard had wanted, before you made an irrevocable decision, her past snickered.

Oh, shut up, she fired back, thinking that Fate was ever fickle. Right now, she had no choice but to keep forging on. For the sake of her children and, now, for her husband's legacy, she needed to keep the farce going for just a bit longer.

Chuck it up to penance, her past chided.

Gabriela flipped her past the figurative finger.

Score: One, for her.

Tires squealed on asphalt from taking the curve too tightly. Startled, she slammed the brakes. The car responded slower than before.

"Mannie, I'm going to kill you if this car needs to go back to your garage."

The venting out loud, however, made her feel better. Definitely. She would call her mechanic and let him have an earful, something similar to the earful she'd received last night from, what was this idiot of a person's name? Wickeham. God. Did she really need this now? The man was obsessed with snatching her rendition of an illustrated medieval manuscript before it went up for auction. At all costs. He kept calling her, insisting she sell her work for a fraction of what she knew it would be worth. Sounded like a professional nagger, raised finger and all. Suggestive, rather than threatening, which irritated the hell out of her. She better sell, or she'd be sorry. Yadda yadda. Arrogant gall.

But therein, possibly, lay the reason for the extended boxing match with her past today. The parallels to some events four years ago were just too damn close. Too damn déjà vuish.

No wonder her past had a smirk on its face. The odds were stacked in its favor.

The gradient on the southbound road turned steep and the car swerved heavily to the right. That snapped her completely out of her self-commiseration.

Taking a steadying breath, she pushed down on the brakes and prepared to downshift to first. The car didn't even hiccup. She pumped the brakes, thinking she had misjudged. Nothing. Her foot went all the way down to the floorboard and stayed there.

Gabriela froze. For an instant, her brain refused to capture the enormity of her current problem. Her muscles didn't twitch and she didn't breathe. *No, this is simply not happening to me. There's a mistake.* She released and pushed once more. The brake pedal slid down in slow motion.

All the way down. No resistance.

It stayed there.

She was *not* wrong.

Oh. My. God.

The sudden influx of adrenaline surged through her body like a savage beast set loose on a hunt after a famine. Her heart hammered her rib cage. Her eyes, hoping something, anything, would help her, darted frantically around. What was she going to do? She had a fifty-foot drop on one side of this two-lane road and a granite wall on the other. Traffic would get heavier as she went lower. Sweat pooled on her inner elbows and nape. She was in serious trouble.

The car sped up.

She started hyperventilating.

Take a deep breath...stay with me, Gabriela. I need you to guide me.

Richard.

The thought of him fighting another car, on another road, somehow steadied her. She rammed the clutch and shifted to first. The car bucked. Almost stalled. Her seat belt bit into her shoulder and torso, and the whine from the motor became a distressing grating of metal. Did the car just slow down a bit? Concentrate, damn it. Concentrate. The next obstacle, the road ahead, was a hair-raiser. It veered away from the drop at a tight angle and twisted back immediately toward the western horizon, the ocean, and the road below.

Prioritize. Slow down the beast. One sucky situation at a time.

Gabriela eased the car into the median, giving herself more driving room. "Please, please," she begged no one in particular. "Don't let anyone come my way."

Tires screeched as she started the turn. Her hands slipped as she maneuvered the steering wheel with the small up-and-down jerks she remembered Richard using. But the car felt heavy, like a lumbering beast wading through thick mud, resisting her directions and weaving farther to the edge of the road. She increased her movements on the steering wheel. The car's rear dragged heavily to the right. Her first instinct was to compensate. She tamped down on that gut move quickly. Defensive driving taught overcompensating would trigger a dangerous spin.

She needed to break the car's momentum before she reached the next turn, the one facing the ocean. She grabbed the emergency brake lever and eased it up a fraction at a time as she kept turning. An acrid smell filtered into the car, but she ignored it. Her eyes scanned the road ahead. No oncoming northbound traffic, yet. Gabriela swallowed and steered diagonally to the opposite side of the road. Horns blared behind her, drivers frantic to get her attention.

She ignored them and concentrated on the approaching section of mountain.

She didn't quite ram the car against the granite, but rather scraped the entire driver side into the rock. Steel and granite pushed against each other. The car bumped once, refusing to stay parallel to the stone. Her side mirror snapped and slammed into her window. Glass cracked. She cringed and gave a frightened squeal. But she forced the car back to the granite. Metal ground against stone, filing the car's exterior like a fingernail. The steering wheel vibrated, hard, and with it her forearms. Keep the car steady became her mantra, despite sweaty hands, despite them slipping on the steering wheel. She increased the pressure on the leather there. *Oh, God. Oh, God.* The car would be pulp before she finished.

More cars blared horns, accelerated, and zipped past her. She caught a brief glimpse of a man gesticulating frantically while on his cell phone. Must think she was crazy, drunk, or high. Hysterical laughter bubbled up but came out as a keening wail.

Oh, God. Oh, God. She needed to stop the car or she was going to die.

Made in the USA
Columbia, SC
14 July 2022

63467514R00070